ROYAL LINE

A Tattered Royals Novel

CARRIE ANN RYAN
NANA MALONE

ROYAL LINE
A TATTERED ROYALS NOVEL

By

Carrie Ann Ryan & Nana Malone

Royal Line
A Tattered Royals Novel
By: Carrie Ann Ryan & Nana Malone
© 2021 Carrie Ann Ryan & Nana Malone
eBook ISBN: 978-1-950443-44-4
Paperback ISBN: 978-1-950443-45-1

Cover Art by Sweet N Spicy Designs
Photograph by Wander Photography

To Nana.
Yes, I get to dedicate this to you, because I got here first.
~Carrie Ann

ROYAL LINE

A princess on the run finds her version of a prince in this epic beginning to the Tattered Royals stand-alone series.

I never asked for my tiara.

My dreams were always bigger than a palace. They're as big as the world.

Being fourth in line for the throne should have guaranteed me freedom.

I thought I was one step from walking away forever, but a long-forgotten rule forces me to run instead.

I refuse to marry a Duke and bear an heir to save our titles.

I trust my brothers to find a way to save my future, but first I need to save myself.

Only I never expected to meet danger...and Kannon Adams along the way.

I never asked for her.

My security business has secured all the clueless princess types I can handle.

Princess London Waterford of Alden is a whole other level of trouble.

Not to mention gorgeous and tempting as royal sin. Too bad she's also in danger.

When the bullets fly, I trust no one else to protect her, even if she pushes me away.

Together, we must find who's behind the threat to her life and try not to get caught in the crossfire.

One night together might never be enough, but if those who want her dead have a say, it'll be our last.

Chapter 1
LONDON

Heavy is the head that wears the tiara.

IN THE DARK, WITH ONLY THE MOONLIGHT TO GUIDE me, my shoes made barely a sound on the cobblestones. The slight chill in the spring air sent a cascade of goosebumps over my skin even as I hustled out of the palace.

My heart rate increased as I forced my breath to even out. If I got caught, it would be bad. *Very* bad. As in, find out if Alden had dungeons bad.

It's not a mistake. You know what you're doing. You know why you're doing it. You just need to make it to the car.

Behind me there is the echo of footsteps, the *clip-*

clop sound echoing against the walls of the palace and the exterior buildings. With each staccato step, they drew nearer, and my heart threatened to race right out of my chest.

I whirled on the shadow chasing me. "I swear to God, Kate, you have to be quieter."

My childhood friend blinked dark eyes at me. "You can't be serious. When you said you had something important to do and you needed my help, I didn't think you meant tonight."

I'd needed help since I knew there was no way I'd be able to get all my equipment out of my room, down the passageways and tunnels, and all the way to the parking lot by myself...unseen. And now it seemed like I might not have asked the right person.

I sighed and took my rolling suitcase from her. "Look, I get it. This makes you really uncomfortable. Have I mentioned what a great friend you are? You're a star. And if you start having second thoughts, just remember, this job is important. There are people counting on me to get to Brazil. It's an amazing opportunity. And on top of that, I actually get to do some good."

I hitched a thumb back toward the palace ballroom. "In there, yes, there's duty and tradition, but I'm not doing any good. Not any *real* good anyway. I'm bound by my place in the hierarchy. In Brazil it's hands-on.

And it's important. It's all I've ever wanted to do. So please try and understand."

She sighed. Her thick auburn hair was coiled into a smooth chignon, and her dark eyes softened as she spoke. "I understand. You've been obsessed with being a photographer since you were little and your mom would take you out on photo excursions. I get that since she died, you've been obsessed with picking up her mantle. Taking on the dream that she had to give up by marrying a prince. But honestly, London. Your brother forbade this."

"And," I whispered as I lugged my bag past the stables, down toward the north parking lot right by the visitor's gates, "when he forbade it, he didn't give me a good reason. It's not like I'm needed here. Between Roman, Breck, and Wilder, they have duty and honor handled. My only role here is to sit around and look pretty if Aunt Rebecca is to be believed. And I can do so much more than that. Have so much more impact than that."

Kate's dark eyes met mine. They were filled with worry and exasperation. We'd grown up together. Our mothers had been close. We'd gone to all the same boarding schools. Had all the same friends.

I'd leaned on her a lot after Mom died. And in turn had held her hand when her father passed away two years ago. I'd also threatened to maim and dismember

Jamison Croft, the financier who had broken her heart. Or rather their engagement. But I knew her heart had always belonged to my brother, Wilder.

It didn't matter how much Wilder doted on her like a little sister. Rubbed her head like she was one of the lads. She still looked at him like the sun shined out of his rear end.

I knew she couldn't understand what I was doing or why I was doing it. Kate loved the pomp and circumstance of the court. And for the most part, I loved the tradition too. But some of the rules just didn't make sense.

For so long, I'd wanted to please my brothers. I wanted to do all the right things. But there were moments when I felt like I was choking on all the right things. There were moments when I knew doing the right thing would require breaking a rule or two.

And tonight was one of those moments. I'd been given a photography assignment as a junior stringer for the BBC's environmental division. I'd applied under one of my aliases. To them, I was London Smith. Plain Jane photographer from Sydney. For the most part we corresponded online, and nobody was the wiser. And I loved it.

By and large, if I was traveling out of Alden, I'd notify the team, tell them where I was going, and I would be given small assignments. It was always a bit tricky trying to do those assignments with constant bodyguards in tow. But I'd managed it pretty well for the last nine months.

But this was my first major assignment. I was being sent to Brazil to photograph Immanuel Sosa, the newest mayor of Sao Paolo, about his Green Earth initiatives. It was my chance to really prove myself. But somehow, Roman had gotten wind of it before I'd even been able to present my case.

I still didn't know how he'd managed that.

A week ago, he'd come to me and told me not to even think about it. We had words, and then, like some kind of authoritarian dictator, he'd told me to know my place. *My place.* My brother, who I loved with all my heart, had looked me in the eye and told me it was for my own good to stay put. For my own good to do as I was told. For my own good to give up this dream. And I knew that I couldn't.

It didn't matter that I knew he was doing it only to keep me safe after we'd lost so much, but it didn't make it *right*.

Mom had walked away from her dreams for love. Dad had given up his dreams for duty.

I was their *fourth* child. I had three older brothers. They had the duty thing down pat. And I knew my parents would be proud of me. Mom in particular. She'd always encouraged me to make my own way. Encouraged me to follow my own dreams.

But then they died.

And everyone had rallied around us like we had to be protected and, in my case, cosseted.

The most difficult part was that I *knew* Roman would be proud when he eventually saw the photos. He'd once told me my photos always reminded him of Mom. If I could just get to Brazil.

Kate must have realized I was making some good points. She tried another tactic. "Do you really intend on missing your own birthday party? Your aunt worked so hard on all the details to make them perfect."

We finally reached the parking lot, and I sighed with relief. My roller bag was heavy, but God, my camera kit with every single lens I owned dug into my shoulder. "Kate, let's be clear, she planned this whole party to impress King Gustav from Sweden. Remember three months ago when I said that I didn't want to have a party and I would much rather have vacationed with my brothers and you? And she made that face that said, but King Gustav will be here this week. That it was important that we did something to commemorate his visit. It happens to look important if he's invited to one of our birthdays."

Kate winced. "Fair enough. Yes. This party is probably mostly for King Gustav. But you're expected there."

"I'm expected, but no one is going to notice if I'm not there. It's really all about King Gustav anyway. Birthday be damned. I love you for making sure I got to the car. But honestly, you don't have to drive me to the airport. I'll just park in long-term parking."

She bit her bottom lip and started to pick at her cuticle, a long-ago nervous habit I knew she hadn't managed to break since we were kids.

I saw it as I heaved my massive camera bag over my shoulder. "Thank you for worrying. But you know as well as I do that no one up there is going to even notice I'm gone."

"Your brothers will notice."

I reached the car with a sigh of relief. I specifically asked for the Peugeot or something reasonably priced. Nothing flashy. Nothing noticeable. I knew if I took the armor-plated Range Rover that Roman made me drive under normal circumstances, I would most certainly be noticed.

I hit the key fob to open up the boot and then loaded my camera bag and my rolling bag into the back. Then I turned to hug Kate. "I'll be home soon. My phone is on, so Roman can call and yell at me whenever he wants."

She sighed. "London, I—"

The passenger side door to the car swung open, and I jumped back. "Oh my God."

My brother Wilder unfolded his long legs to stand at

full height. In the moonlight, his midnight-black hair looked almost blue. "Going somewhere, little sis?"

I turned to glare at Kate with wide eyes. "You didn't." I knew that she had. She was unable to deny Wilder anything.

"London, I'm sorry, but you were going to get in trouble. And Wilder said this was in your best interest."

"I can't believe you did this."

"I'm sorry. But I was worried. If you're going to go, you need a full-scale security team. What you're doing is dangerous."

Dangerous, my ass. I couldn't help but wonder what my brother had offered her in exchange. He could be quite persuasive and manipulative—despite the fact that he was the quietest one of the four of us. When I turned my attention back to Wilder, he had his arm propped on the roof of the car. "A Peugeot? Really, London? You should have at least taken the Mercedes."

I lifted my chin to glower at my brother. His snobbery knew no bounds. "What are the chances I can bribe you not to tell Roman?"

He merely chuckled. "I'm not going to tell him." Hope bloomed in my chest, spreading slowly out to my extremities. Was I going to get away with this? Would it be possible to still make my escape? But then he dashed all hope. "You're going to do the honors. As soon as you get ready for the party. Your guests are waiting."

"Wilder!"

But there was no swaying him once his mind was made up. "You know how Roman is, between the paparazzi weirdos and the general lack of security. You knew this was going to happen."

Last ditch, London. Make it good. "Well, it could still happen if you let me go."

He lifted his brow, his blue eyes telling me what I knew in my soul. I wouldn't be making my escape tonight. I was going to go back upstairs and put on the pretty blue frock that would bring out my eyes.

I would do as I was told. There would be no dreaming today.

There'd be no dreaming tomorrow.

And possibly no dreaming ever.

IF I WERE TO THROW MY TIARA ACROSS THE ROOM, would it cut anyone?

If no one cared enough to listen, would it make a sound as it slid across the floor, metal and jewels against marble tile?

And if I were to complain to anyone about the fact that I had to wear a damn tiara to this function, I might as well write *first world problem* in permanent marker on my forehead and figure out how to kick my own ass.

"Princess London, why is such a beautiful girl as you, standing alone in the corner?"

I held back a biting remark that, at the age of twenty-nine—as of today—I was a woman, not a girl, but I refrained. Snapping at random people who were just trying to be pleasant to me on my birthday just wasn't done.

"Hello, there. I was merely taking a moment to myself." I plastered a pleasant smile on my face and turned to the handsome gentleman at my side. He had dark hair, a chiseled jaw, and a smile that would drop the panties of half the women in the ballroom.

I wasn't one of those women tonight, and probably never would be.

"Ah, sorry to bother you then." He bowed low. "Happy birthday, Princess. I do believe we'll talk again soon." On that cryptic comment, he walked away, leaving me wondering if I was missing something.

"What's with the snarl?"

I blinked and looked over at my brother Breck, who just smiled at me. The familiar twinkle in his eyes reminded me that I was home, even if I would rather be out with the rest of the world, not pretending like I actually had a right to be here among people who did so much more with their lives than I did.

"I am not snarling. Princesses do not snarl."

"No, they smile daintily and nod their little heads

while they curtsy, and they also use big scissors to cut through ribbons when they open up buildings."

"And what do princes do?" I asked, doing my best to hold back a smile. It was not good to encourage him, but I couldn't help it. I loved my brother, even if he was a bit much to handle.

"Princes smirk, they bow, they kiss princesses' hands," he said, lifting my hand to give my knuckles a brush of his lips. "And they wink," he added.

"They wink," I said. "And that is the best you can come up with?"

"I've had short notice. I promise I will come up with something better in the future. Just give me time."

"And yet, it always feels like I'm running out of time." I hadn't meant to say the words aloud, but there was no taking them back.

"What's wrong? Talk to me."

I shook my head. How could I make him understand? "Nothing, I guess. Just having a rough day."

"It's your birthday party. You are the center of attention, the literal belle of the ball. You're home in Alden, in the palace our forebears shed their blood, sweat, and tears for to create their own kingdom."

"I'm pretty sure there are a few oxymorons in that statement."

"Why do I feel like there was an implicit 'moron' in that remark?" he asked with a smirk.

Brothers and princes, you didn't know what to do with them until it was too late.

I could do this. Put on the happy face for him. "I will smile, and I will laugh, and I will eat cake, and I will enjoy myself. I just needed a minute to act like a spoiled princess and sulk in a corner."

"You don't need to hide yourself from me."

I didn't think that was actually the case. I hid myself from everyone. That was how I got things done. And I knew for a fact that Breck, and my other brothers, Wilder and Roman, hid as well.

That's what made us royals. We hid from the public, and sometimes from ourselves, but we got things done.

And we helped our people.

And that was enough of that.

"Okay, I want cake."

"That's my girl. First, you must dance, cake is much later. Aunt Rebecca wouldn't allow us to cut the cake too early." Breck screwed up his face when he mimicked her voice. "That just isn't done."

Laughing, I rolled my eyes as I slid my hand into his, following him out onto the dance floor, my dress swinging around my ankles as others joined us.

"Why do we let her run everything?"

Breck twirled me around the polished marble, demonstrating the three-times-a-week dance lessons that had been forced on him as a child.

"Because she helped raised us, because she has been the one organizing the social schedules of the kingdom since we lost our parents, and because if you don't *let* her do something, she'll do it anyway and scold you about it, all with a polite smile."

I laughed at that, ignoring the warning look from one of the husbands of a councilwoman who didn't like the idea of royals amongst them. It might be my birthday, but they were sure to remind me that they paid for everything and I was just a pretty princess on a cloud with no job and no prospects.

What was with me tonight?

I pushed those thoughts out of my head and turned back to Breck. "Oh leave her alone. Aunt Rebecca doesn't snap. Or yell. She's...kind." And pushy and overbearing, but I didn't say those things. My brothers had, of course, had to deal with Aunt Rebecca's needling and orders as she helped raise us. But as we had all said before, it was for our own good. Truth be told, she was a larger part of my life than my brothers were. They had been well into their teen years when my parents died.

We had lost our parents long ago, and when Roman became king, we had been shoved to the front of the news, the country, and into the eyes of the world. And Aunt Rebecca had been there in the wings, waiting, making sure we were taken care of. And I would never be able to thank her enough.

There was always a part of me that wanted to be somewhere else. Even if it wasn't grateful or what a princess would do.

"How is planning for the trip?"

I shrugged. "I'm still not sure I'm going." I held back a growl since my latest attempt had once again been thwarted.

"What? Why? You should go," Breck said, as if he could read my mind.

"We both know Roman won't let me." And he'd already sent his henchman, aka our brother, to make sure I couldn't.

"You've been mumbling about this project for how long? Just do it."

"Working princesses can't be travel photojournalists. I want to go out and experience the real world, and not from behind bulletproof glass or with pearls around my neck. I want to get to know what's truly beneath the surface, and I can't do that. It's just not done."

"And when has that ever stopped a Waterford before?" Breck asked, that haughty tone back in his voice that made me smile.

"We always do what's expected of us."

"If that were the case, Roman would be married."

I gave my brother a sharp look, and he had the grace to wince. "Sorry. I don't know where that came from."

"We'll all do what we need to do, what's expected, but you know as well as I do that Roman's not ready."

"When is he going to be, L?"

Luckily the waltz ended. I shook my head and moved off the dance floor as the music shifted to a more upbeat song.

"Let's talk about something happier. It's my birthday. I should be happy."

From behind me, someone said, "It is your birthday. Last one before you hit the big 3-0."

I turned to find my other brother, Wilder, and smiled, holding out my arms as if I hadn't just seen him a few hours earlier. He hugged me tight, kissing the top of my head, and I sank into his hold. I knew I shouldn't have favorites, but Wilder had always been mine—even if I hated him just a little bit for not letting me leave as of yet. Maybe if wasn't for the party, he'd have helped me live my dream. I had to believe that. But for now, I was still hurt about the whole thing.

All my brothers were big, muscular, and handsome as sin, according to the tabloid magazines and paparazzi that hounded us. Each of them had dark hair and light, bright eyes that seemed to shine in every photo.

People said I looked like them, but I didn't agree. Their eyes were just a bit brighter, their hair a bit shinier. And maybe it was because I was the baby sister who always saw my brothers as larger than life.

After all, they were literal princes. What else could they be in my eyes?

"We're not supposed to call her old yet," Breck said, leaning toward me as he stood by Wilder. The two were a sight for sure, and one of the ladies passing noticed. She practically tripped over her feet.

"We're not supposed to call me old, ever." I snapped it out, but the boys didn't listen. They never did.

"Well, if she's old, then so are we," Wilder said.

"No, we're men. We age like a fine whiskey."

"And what am I?" I asked, my hands on my hips. I might have a tiara on my head and silk and lace wrapped around my body, but I would throw down right here and tackle my brother if I had to.

Just because I might own night cream didn't mean I was ready for dotage. I knew they were just teasing me, but I loved trading barbs with them.

"Why are the three hosts of this party standing in a corner and not socializing?" a deep voice asked from behind me.

I turned, a tentative smile on my face. "Roman."

"Happy birthday, baby sister," my brother said as he leaned down and brushed a small kiss on my cheek. He looked every bit the king he was.

It was a breach of proper etiquette, but it was my birthday, and the king did break the rules sometimes. Or perhaps he just bent them to his will with his fierce gaze and that stern frown that was perpetually on his face.

"We're just deciding which of us is going to start getting wrinkles first," Breck said.

"Well it's already you, isn't it?" Wilder asked while Breck frowned.

"Not me. If anything, it's going to be Roman here. Old man."

I was the baby sister of four, with Wilder being only a year older than me, and Breck being a couple of years older than that. But Roman had a larger gap in age than the rest of us.

Our parents had loved each other, had a whirlwind romance, and had been amongst the greatest kings and queens of the ages, according to Alden's history.

When we lost them, the world had mourned.

But before that happened, they'd had four children. Each one brought into the world with love, light, and paparazzi flashes in their eyes.

I wasn't a fan of the latter and considering what I wanted to be instead of a princess, it made sense.

I was a photographer. Not a princess in my head all the time.

I wanted to find a blend of both, one where I could see through the lens and take pictures of the world and understand human nature and nature itself.

I wanted to do all of that and see the world without

CARRIE ANN RYAN & NANA MALONE

having a bodyguard at my side or a royal reason for being there.

Wishes didn't make choices, and unless I stood up for myself and finally asked, it was never going to happen.

"Come with me," Roman said, frowning.

I looked at Breck and Wilder, who just shrugged, and we followed the King of Alden out of the room, wondering what on earth he could have to say to us tonight.

"What is it? You were just meeting with the King of Sweden, right? Nothing could have happened there," Breck said.

"I like Sweden," Wilder said.

"As do I, hence why nothing would happen to occasion this meeting."

"You can't go," Roman said.

I froze, my hands fisting in front of me. "Excuse me?" I turned away from him, looked at my other brothers, then turned back. "How does everyone know what I want to do before I even say it?"

"We have our ways. This trip of yours is going to be too dangerous. I know you want to go and take photos and do something that you're passionate about, but you can't. It's too dangerous considering the times we're in. I'm sorry. But I forbid it."

Rage curled in my belly, and I swallowed hard, trying to understand exactly what he had just said.

"You're forbidding it?"

"Roman," Wilder whispered.

"Really? That's the line you're taking?" Breck asked in a quiet voice.

"I can forbid whatever the hell I want to. I am the King of Alden. I am *your* king."

"You are my brother, you might be my king, but you are not my owner and not my father."

He didn't wince at the reminder of what we'd lost, but I saw his eyes narrow infinitesimally.

"No, I'm not either of those things, but I am your ruler. You have a job here. You are to act in place of my queen until it is deemed that I find a queen of my own. You have duties here that you are neglecting every time you see fit to leave this kingdom on another jaunt of yours."

"Really? A jaunt. It's a job. An actual job. One where I'm not cutting ribbons and smiling for people instead of doing what I want."

"Then find something that you like to do *here*. Be someone. Make a contribution. But I can only keep you safe if you're here."

Breck and Wilder just stood with their mouths agape, but I was shaking. I couldn't think. I couldn't breathe.

Before I could say anything in rebuttal, heels clattered on the marble floor behind us, and I whirled to see Aunt Rebecca running in, her face pale, her hands on her dress, lifting her skirts so she wouldn't trip.

Aunt Rebecca never ran. She was always poised and in control, her royal majesty in all but name. She would have been an amazing queen if she had not been born second to my father.

"Roman, you must listen."

"I'm busy. I can't meet with the council right now. I just got back into the country, and it's London's birthday. We're celebrating."

"Some celebration," I mumbled.

"I know you're busy, but you must listen." A chill of foreboding slid over my body as I narrowed my eyes at her, the tone of her voice one I hadn't heard in far too long.

"Listen to what?" I asked carefully.

"London, if you run off and chase your dreams and neglect your duties, you'll lose your throne. And Roman, you'll lose everything."

Chapter 2
LONDON

Royal lines never fade. Memories do.

"WHAT THE FUCK ARE YOU TALKING ABOUT, AUNT Rebecca?" Roman's voice boomed, causing it to echo off of the walls in his study. It was unusual that my brother lost his temper. He was always so self-contained. This was the first time I'd seen absolute fury on his face.

Our aunt didn't cower though. She stood her ground and lifted her chin. The trembling in her hands was the only thing that belied her fear. "Don't shoot the messenger, Roman. I'm sorry to interrupt, but you need to know this because I'm trying to help."

Her words seemed to calm Roman down, and I stepped forward and grabbed her arm.

He tried again. "Sorry, Aunt Rebecca. What's going on?"

She patted my hand. "London, sweetheart, I'm sorry to do this on your birthday, but I've only just been made aware of it." Her gaze flickered around to meet each of ours. "An emergency appeal was brought to the council tonight."

Roman's voice was still tight. "What kind of emergency appeal?"

Aunt Rebecca licked her lips, her makeup so expertly done it almost masked the lines around her mouth. "There is an obscure law that has never been used before until now. The law states that there must be a child born to the royal line before the last child in that line reaches thirty. I'm so sorry, darlings. You know I'd never want to see this happen to any of you. I love you all so much."

A nervous laugh bubbled out of my throat. "What? That's ridiculous."

"I agree," Aunt Rebecca said. "But it's one of those things that was likely brought about to enforce alliances with neighboring kingdoms to ensure that there was always new royal blood." At my stricken expression, she squeezed my hand. "I'm sorry. I didn't know."

My brother Wilder shook his head. "No, there's no

way. How in the world did this happen, and why didn't we know?" He tilted his chin up at Roman. "You're the king. Change the rule."

Roman's expression was tight, and the muscle in his jaw ticked. "You know full well I can't just change a law. It requires the Council of Lords to vote. And they're not due to meet for another month. Obviously, London has just turned twenty-nine. That gives us a year to figure out what to do."

What the hell were they talking about? No way could they be entertaining any of this. A hysterical laugh bubbled up. "You guys, what the hell am I supposed to do if you can't get the law changed? Get married, get knocked up, and have a baby just so you lot can rule? No, thank you."

Aunt Rebecca took both my hands. "Look, it's not going to come to that, okay? I have a plan. First, we'll go to the Council of Lords like your brother said, okay?"

The squeeze of her hands was soothing. Calming. Ever since Mom died, Aunt Rebecca had stepped up so often to help, to keep me calm. Growing up in a family of men was difficult. But she was always there. "Look, I will make this right, okay?"

From the corner, Breck watched us all. "This is bull-shit. You can't make London have a baby. Her womb isn't up for auction."

Aunt Rebecca turned to him. "*I* know that. And *you*

know that. But the laws are the laws, and we still need the Council of Lords to change them."

Roman rubbed his jaw. "All right. Aunt Rebecca, can you convene an emergency council meeting? We need to resolve this quickly."

"Yes, I will. But also, I have another solution."

Roman's brows drew down. "What do you mean?"

"Well, just in case, we can help London find someone."

Breck snorted. "Have you met London? Her dating life is a disaster under the best of circumstances. What? You're going to find a ready-made royal somewhere who is her type? Which means, really, too pretty to be useful for anything. He has to be eccentric and quirky and like going on adventures with her. Oh, and we have to approve of him. Good luck, Auntie."

Aunt Rebecca released my hands and crossed her arms. "Well, are you offering a solution? I have someone London could meet. She's actually met him once or twice already. He's lovely. You spoke to him tonight, even."

Roman's eyes went wide. "You're serious? You're proposing we marry London off?"

"Well, none of you seem to be doing your duty. And Roman, honestly, I know how difficult things have been for you. But you left it too long, and now it's up to your sister. Can any of you have a baby?"

My brothers all shuffled on their feet. *Assholes.* "Aunt Rebecca, I love you, but it's not happening." I gestured toward my lower belly. "Nothing is coming to live here. It's inhospitable. Babies don't go well with photojournalism."

She gave me a soft smile. "I know. But we are in a tight spot now. We'll try and get the law changed, but we need to prepare ourselves while we still can."

Roman shook his head. "London, don't worry. We'll make sure this doesn't happen."

"Roman, I appreciate you wanting to protect her," Aunt Rebecca said. "But you have to understand, since an emergency appeal was put forth, she has to show that she's taking this seriously. Otherwise, the Council of Lords will be against her. If she's making no effort, there are those on the Council who will think that you're trying to skirt them."

Roman lifted a shoulder in a nonchalant shrug. "I *am* trying to skirt them."

"You can't. Or at least you can't be seen as doing so. We have to follow the rules until we can get them changed or re-assessed. London, it's in your best interest to announce your engagement posthaste."

My jaw unhinged. "Engagement?"

"Well, yes. If you meet the duke and he's at least good-looking enough for you, we can start those proceedings and then show good faith... Like you know the rule, you understand the rule, and you're willing to play ball. And then when we get it changed, you won't have to get married."

"I'm not marrying someone I don't love."

She sighed. "Sweetheart, you know full well that many royal marriages are not about love."

"I'm the girl. I don't have to fulfill the duty. It's Roman's job. And Breck is right behind him. Why do I have to be involved? You can't sell me off to the highest bidder."

Aunt Rebecca huffed. "I'm not *selling* you. We have hard truths to deal with right now. What else can we do?"

Breck gasped. "Wait, so the next line, that's...bloody Barkley?"

Aunt Rebecca winced. "I think everyone in this room knows what would happen to the throne if my son sat on it."

My brothers all grimaced. Another hysterical laugh bubbled out of me. "Jesus Christ, is this for real?"

My aunt nodded. "Unfortunately, yes."

My brothers and I just stared at each other miserably.

"Look, I'm going to go speak to some of the lords in attendance and let them know we need to have an emergency session in the morning. Roman, you might as well get some notes prepared on why we're not going to allow this to occur. Even offer up Wilder and Breck if you have to. Something. Anything. We have to stop this."

Tears welled in my eyes. There was no fucking way. I was not getting engaged to some random duke, and I was certainly not having a baby. I had plans. Things I needed to do. I didn't even want to be a royal. So why the hell did I have to suck it up and fulfill the duty? Just so my brothers didn't have to? "Aunt Rebecca, thank you. What would I do without you?"

She smoothed her hand over my cheek, her thumb caressing my cheekbone. "You'll never have to find out. I'll take care of this, okay?"

When she left, I turned around and leaned against the door. "I cannot do this. I'm not getting married. Not to some random duke. I want love. I deserve that."

Roman sighed. "Relax, I'm not going to let it happen."

"Okay, then who's it going to be who's popping out an heir? It's not you, Roman, for obvious reasons."

Breck pepped up. "Listen, I don't even have anyone on the horizon to marry. Can you imagine me married?"

I rolled my eyes in disgust. There were stories about how Breck lived up to his reputation constantly. So many rumors in fact that I shuddered just thinking of one.

"Roman, I *can't*."

"And you don't have to. I'm not going to let it happen."

Breck stepped forward. "All right, so she obviously can't get married to some random duke. What are we going to do?"

Roman scrubbed his hand over his face. "Well, for starters, she's going to get the hell out of Dodge."

My mouth fell open. "Roman, Mr. Follow the Rules, what are you going to do, squirrel me out of here? Didn't you just forbid me from living my life not thirty minutes ago?"

"If I didn't, you would just go on your own, right?"

"Do you have a point?"

Breck clapped his hands together. "All right, someone hand me my laptop. I can mess with the cameras to make it look like she's in her room, at least through the morning. I'll buy her some time. You'll need cash and documents."

"We'll find you a safe house. There are many on the council who are loyal to us. They were loyal to Mom and Dad. They'll help. They'll stall the vote until we can find a loophole."

I blinked at my brothers. "You're serious? You're going to help me?"

Roman's brow furrowed. "Did you think that we wouldn't?"

I lifted a shoulder. "I don't know. You like being a king."

"*Like* is the wrong word for it. But no way in hell will I allow Barkley to take this throne. Or anyone else for that matter. I care about the people more than I care about being king. But right now, my personal interests are in line with the common good, so come on. I'll figure out a way to get you the hell out of here."

Roman went to the safe behind the massive painting of our parents. "Before they died, Mom and Dad were clear that we all should always have multiple passports. Yours are in here."

"How is this my life right now?"

"Better you do it with help than on your own."

Wilder nodded. "I have a list of safe houses we can send her to. America. Hell, let's go farther. Australia. Ooh, we have Tonga."

Roman shook his head. "No, she can't be anywhere that the lords would know because they would summon her right back."

"Oh wait," I offered. "Remember my friend, Rian? She lives in Paris. I can stay with her. We've been friends since boarding school. No one knows her."

Wilder stroked his jaw, rubbing at his stubble. "That might work, actually. Does she have security?"

"I— I don't know."

He shook his head. "Don't worry. Breck, see if you

can find her security company and tap into their systems. See if she's got any security."

"Well, she's an actress, so she probably does, in order to protect herself," I said.

Roman stiffened at that. "Wait, *that* Rian?"

"Yes. You met her once when you came to pick me up at school."

He swallowed hard then. *What was wrong with him?*

Breck nodded. "She has a decent security system in her country flat. It's basic but a little more upgraded. Panic room and everything. It's a good place to hide out until we figure this out."

Roman handed me the passports. "You've got a couple of options there. One is American, which is great because it's from when you went to boarding school, and you can pull off the accent." He handed the little portfolios to me, and I stared down at them. Next, he handed me cash.

Wilder rolled his eyes and stepped into the safe and pulled out a bag. It was a cross-body situation that looked sturdy but slightly fashionable. "Here, use this."

I shoved the passports into it. The money was harder.

Wilder said, "This backpack should do. We'll pack you a few sets of clothes, but you're going to have to borrow. You want to travel as light as possible right now."

Breck tapped away on his laptop. "I've already got her on a charter flight to Paris using the name on the passport."

I glanced around at my brothers. "Oh my God, you guys are insane, but I love you."

Roman pulled me in for a tight hug, and I almost didn't know what to do. He never touched people, but slowly my arms wrapped around him. He felt solid and warm, like home. He smelled so familiar, just like Dad always had. I could have nestled there all day. But too soon, he was shrugging back, pushing me away, and erecting the walls again. "We have to get you out of here."

Wilder nodded. "I've got a way out. There's a tunnel right outside the offices. It'll lead her down to the back exit. I'll drive her to the airport myself."

So this was happening? "I didn't even get my cake."

Roman chuckled. "Eat cake in Paris. Right now, your safety and your freedom are more important than anything."

"You obviously don't know how important a cake is to me."

Breck gave me a tight squeeze and picked me up off the floor. "Look, we'll figure this out. This is just a mini vacation in Paris. How bad could it be?"

His smile was light, but I could see it in his eyes; he was worried.

Roman, gave me another quick squeeze and then stepped back. Wilder put out his hand. "Come on, little sis. Let's get you in the car. Looks like you're getting that adventure you've always wanted after all."

Chapter 3
KANNON

How did it come to this?

A CLIENT, WAS A CLIENT, WAS A CLIENT, WAS A client.

I didn't care what kind of clients we had at Kannon Security. All I cared about was that we had them. And business had been good over the last three years. We'd weathered the rocky storms and growing pains of building a solid security business.

But if I had to rank our clients in a hierarchy of worst to best, my current assignment, Lilith Montague, was the worst kind.

First, she was the daughter of a diplomat. That meant she'd spent most of her life learning how to appear to be one thing while being something else entirely. She'd spent her whole life smiling for the cameras, shaking hands, being the perfect daughter, while behind the scenes, being allowed to get away with murder. Although, I hoped that wasn't literal in this case.

I loathed diplomats' kids because they were the ones most likely to thwart the rules. They threw themselves into finding trouble and not bothering to find their way out of it. And despite access to the finest education, they did their best to squander every single opportunity placed in front of them and pull out that dumbass card every chance they got.

And Lilith Montague was no different. If she heard there was a squander-your-life event, she'd be first in line for that shit. She was your typical Kardashian-living, influencer-aspiring, refuse-to-do-anything-with-the-brain-God-gave-her kind of girl. Which was a shame, because I had a great deal of respect for her father.

Drake Montague had given me my first job. Right after I opened Kannon Security, he'd picked our no-name security firm to do a job for him at an event. I'd asked him why he'd chosen us, and he said because he'd been like me once. Unlike most diplomats, he'd served in the military, and he'd honestly wanted to make the world better.

Thanks to his endorsement, we'd gotten bigger and better contracts. I would always be grateful to him. Especially given the shitstorm of my life before I opened Kannon Security.

When Drake Montague called looking for a favor, I didn't say no.

My other least favorite kind of job was the bodyguard gigs to concerts. The kind of shows that made Burning Man look like a stuffy event. First and foremost, there were drugs everywhere. Too many exits and entrances, and they were always packed to the gills. Not to mention my team basically telegraphed that they were bodyguards. We worked best in casual attire; dressed up, we stood out like sore thumbs. We were the only ones not taking any drugs. It didn't help that everything was brightly lit with flashing lights suffusing the area. It was easy to miss what you needed to see, and far too easy to see something that wasn't there at all.

Sparrow tapped into her coms. "Boss, can you check your south exit? Something looks off."

I frowned at that. "Copy." I headed that way, holding back a growl.

Sparrow made her way to the women's restroom. Her sightline was on Lilith at the bar. And my other guys, Max and Aidan, were basically beating the men off of her. Sparrow at least looked undercover. She looked like she could be one of Lilith's friends. Which certainly helped.

My gaze narrowed, and I frowned when I locked onto what Sparrow had seen at the exit.

"Blue baseball hat, ripped tank, eyes glued on Lilith?"

"Yup, that's the one. He's been keeping a little too close from behind as we've made our rounds. I keep seeing him on my radar."

"Copy. I'll go talk to him."

Normally, with a job like this, I'd send Sparrow with Olly or Marcus. Nikolai worked better on his own. But because this was Drake's daughter, the whole team came along for the ride. *Fantastic.* Not like Drake wasn't paying us handsomely, but still, a babysitting gig. And all said, with all of us here, we were billing at thousands an hour. As if we had no other active pressing cases.

Easy. Drake gave you a shot when you were about to spiral into the depths of hell. So cut the kid some slack.

I had to remind myself of that. Without Drake's support, things would have been much, much worse for me. I could put up with his daughter for a night...at a Paris Fashion Week party.

Suddenly, there was a long beat of silence that sent my arm hairs standing at attention. It was the calm before the storm. Then there was a bass drop accompanied by a loud bullhorn alarm. The kind they played in clubs. Some DJ came on with a mic and said, "We're going to kick it old school, ladies and gents, taking us back and dropping you into a little foam."

I frowned. "Did he just say foam?"

On the other end of the coms, Sparrow made a gagging sound. "Yes, he did. And for the record, I'd like to note that it's disgusting."

Olly laughed. "He is really trying to nail that old-school vibe and kiss the designer's ass. 1999 is the theme of the Blink & Marc fashion show. Weren't any of you paying attention? Sparrow, you of all people."

Sparrow snorted. "Um, no. I don't do the whole fashion thing. I just naturally look fabulous. Besides, check your patriarchy at the door, handsome. It is possible for me to have tits and not like fashion."

"Are you two done yet?" I frowned as I searched the crowd. Luckily, I towered over most of the party guests. "Nikolai, Blue Cap has vanished from sight. I repeat, he's vanished from sight."

I made my way to the door, hoping to catch the guy, but I couldn't find him in the crowd. And then the foam started. Kids at the center of the dance floor started hopping around and slipping. The designers had thrown this little after-party to celebrate the booming success of their line. Frankly, I didn't understand how bright colors and baggy jeans were somehow now *back* in style.

Suddenly, Sparrow's frantic voice came back through the coms with a hint of tension. "Lilith is gone. I can't find her. Vanished in the crowd."

Whiskey Tango Foxtrot? "Repeat?" This couldn't be happening. *No. No. No. No.*

"I repeat, Lilith has gone missing."

"Fan out. Olly and Marcus, put yourselves at the exits. Max and Aiden, east and west stairs. No one walks in or out of here. Sparrow, you start down the north side, work your way to the center, I will follow up from the south." Jesus fucking Christ. "Nikolai, you start in the middle."

This was not happening. I had not lost Drake Montague's daughter, for the love of Christ.

As my team searched frantically, I kept the coms open. My eyes fervently searched the crowd. Every pencil-necked, needle-headed prick who thought he was God's gift to women and used the opportunity with the foam to bump and grind on the girls made it difficult, if not impossible, to see in the crowd.

Lilith had been wearing all white. Some midriff-baring thing with fringe on the bottom of it, and barely-there shorts. Unfortunately, she looked like every other model in here.

We hunted through the crowd, person by person, and I was ready to make the call to shut down the entire after-party when I finally caught sight of a blue cap in the periphery of my vision, heading into the bathroom—or at least into the private VIP bathroom area.

The party was so exclusive that those who were personal friends to the designers got their own VIP area, which meant there were no webcams.

I made my way over there, and an attendant tried to stop me, but I held up my badge. The whole team had gotten them for complete VIP access.

Thanks to years of rigorous training, I'd managed to keep the bulk of my adrenaline at bay. But this woman was slowing down my progress, and I was about to forget to be a gentleman. But luckily, she didn't have to see my grumpy side.

With a grumble, she let me pass. My gaze swept the area over and over, cataloguing and then dismissing everyone in the section.

When I didn't see Lilith or Blue Cap, that left only one place they could be. I pressed my com unit at my shoulder. "Sparrow, stand by for confirmation. I might have located Lilith Montague."

Unlike the main area, the VIP bathrooms were far less crowded. There were only two women waiting, and I caught the eye of the curvy brunette. "Excuse me, have you seen a man about medium height and weight, dark hair, blue baseball cap?"

Her gaze swept over me. "Just when I thought my night was looking up, you go and ask me where another guy went? Bummer. You would have really made my night."

My cheeks heated, but I kept my stern face on. "I promise, I'm not that much fun. Now have you seen him or not?"

With a shrug, she lifted her head toward the bathroom door. "In there with some debutante."

I tested the door to the bathroom, only to find it locked. The same woman who had hit on me told me there were stalls, so why the fuck had Lilith locked the door?

I knelt in front of the knob, pulled out my lock pick set, and had the doorknob turning in seconds.

When I stood and shifted to the side, I found Blue Cap. It turned out, there had been a reason he'd been watching Lilith.

Lilith was perched on top of the counter, her legs wrapped around Blue Cap's waist, grinding her body on his as she snorted white powder off his shoulder.

I tapped my com. "Stand down. I located her."

What I wanted to do was rip her away and warn her that her father was looking for her, but I didn't bother. Instead, I marched back out, closed the bathroom door behind me, and stood watch, wondering how the hell this had become my life.

Her father's directive had been clear. Keep an eye on her. Be discrete. And only intervene if her life was in imminent danger. Apparently, those were the terms Lilith had negotiated with her father, so my hands were tied—no matter how much I wanted to toss Blue Cap out on his ass. I had to stand where I was and hope...and wait.

You know how this happened.

Ordinarily, I refused to let the memories come back. But apparently, I didn't have a choice tonight. With Phoebe gone, I'd had to pick up the pieces. And unfortunately, the price of putting my life back together meant jobs like this.

Sparrow's voice was clear. "You got her, boss?"

"I have her."

"I presume she's alive?"

"Yes. Perfectly fine. She's got a coke habit, but other than that, she's peachy."

"Jesus Christ," she muttered. "Who even does coke anymore?"

"I know. Aren't we the lucky ones?" I muttered.

"All right, where are you? I'll relieve you and take her home."

"No. I've got this. You watch the exits with Olly."

I didn't care who I owed favors to, but I was done with these things from now on. No more babysitting. At least, no more babysitting debutantes. There had to be more to life than this. There just had to.

Chapter 4
KANNON

That was unexpected.

My skin still hummed with adrenaline. When I deposited Little Miss Debutante at the car, Sparrow came over and checked in. "You all right, boss?"

"Fine. Considering that I had been all systems go before realizing the emergency alarms in my brain were nothing more than a debutante meeting her dealer for a requisite line of coke at an event."

She laughed. "Let this be a lesson to you. Debutantes aren't our thing. Women hiding from their husbands, *that's* our lane."

"Well, all of it is part of our job. Besides, the longer we're around, the larger the favors are that get called in."

She cocked her head and gave me a saucy smile. "Then stop giving out IOUs. Just because someone saves your life once or helps you walk across the street after a long day doesn't mean they should command any of your time in the future. Pay them back in kind. With something small. Not like, 'Sure I'll watch your daughter at a big event and make sure no one tries to kill or kidnap her. Oh, and it's okay to neglect to mention that your child is a handful with a coke fiend boyfriend.'"

"Right," I grumbled. "And she was such a sweet kid."

"Take off those rose-colored glasses. They don't look good on you."

"I hear you." But I repaid favors. No matter what.

I let out a sigh and put my mind back on work. I looked at Sparrow and Olly and said, "Get her back to the plane safely. Check in when you're done. And since you've been on it tonight, have Max do the report."

She grinned at me then, and it occurred to me that Sparrow was actually beautiful. Sure, yes, she was attractive. Dark hair, green eyes. Medium-deep skin. Fit. Amazing cheekbones. But beyond the regular physical characteristics, when she smiled, her whole face lit up. And she could warm up a room with that smile alone, but she didn't show it much. Sparrow was my focused one. If shit went down, she was the one I would likely call first. She wasn't my most senior team member, but she was the one who would have the ultimate focus during any mission. She worried about getting the solution first, no emotions. Or at least she kept them tucked neatly away. I respected that.

Like you're an expert at tucking away your emotions.

I was. I could be. Just every now and again, they reared their ugly heads.

"All right, good job today. Check in when you get her on the plane."

"Will do." She wagged her finger at me. "Oh, don't forget to collect the check. That's my favorite part."

I grinned. "I'll admit, it does give me a boost too."

I stood back as Sparrow climbed into the follow car while Olly stayed at Lilith's side as he led her to the limousine. Marcus and Aiden were with Sparrow. Max and Nicolai joined Olly in the Limo. Little Miss Coke-Habit was going nowhere tonight, and her loser boyfriend/dealer certainly wasn't following. Olly and Sparrow would stay in Paris for a few more days to make sure any evidence of Lilith doing anything wild were wiped from all memories and potential mobile phones as well as CCTVs.

"Okay, time for you to get some rest," Sparrow said from the window as she shot me a look that said she was the one in charge of me...which she wasn't. At least, most days.

She had a point, but my system was still charged with adrenaline. Didn't mean I had to like it. I glanced around, sure there must be something else that needed my attention. That was the thing about having a good team. You delegated a lot. And even after a night like tonight when I had to be in attendance because of committed partnerships, it was like my body got geared up for the fight, but then there *was* no fight. So every time I turned around, I expected something to jump out, something to not be right, something to go dreadfully wrong. But still...*nothing*.

I headed to the east parking lot, passing women in their fashion-forward glitterati outfits. Some with barely-there swathes of fabric covering nipples and snatches. Others wore flowing evening gowns but with daring-enough slits to make a man look twice. And still others had that fashion-forward vibe but were more covered up. That was the life of fashion shows. Everyone dripped in diamonds, smelled of the most expensive perfumes, and had more skin than clothing showing.

Most of the women had on so much makeup that I had no idea what they actually looked like under all the war paint. Were they that tanned? Or was that healthy glow thanks to a good contourist? Was that even what they were called? Who the fuck knew?

I found my black BMW i8 Roadster right where I'd left it, and I couldn't help but do a sweep around the car. Checked the undercarriage, searched for explosives, double-checked that everything was, in fact, as I'd left it.

Old habits died hard. Besides, those old habits kept people alive.

Not always.

I swallowed the bite of guilt and regret, used my fingerprint to open my door, and climbed in. There was a sense of familiarity in the car. It was ridiculous to have it flown over for just two weeks, but I'd been hoping for the opportunity to take a few days off and have a drive. It was always best with your own wheels. Getting it shipped back home would take a lot longer, so I'd have to use one of the company cars until then. But it was well worth the luxury of having it in Paris.

At the security exit, I pulled out my ticket, showed them my ID badge, and then was waved through. I drove out onto the teeming streets of Paris. The city was bustling. The venue was a stately affair. Lit up elegantly. The Carrousel du Louvre was the historic primary location of Paris Fashion Week. Every night, the streets of Paris filled with people. Many stopped to take photos in front of the Louvre. Models teetering on their heels like the leggy giraffes they were.

I knew for a fact that Fashion Week wasn't over. There were more parties, more places to see and be seen. Luckily, I didn't have to do any of that. I headed out of the central part of the city and away from all the people.

After all, it was Paris, so there were people everywhere all the time. I took my car toward the 16th arrondissement. I was familiar enough with the city to know where I was going without needing GPS. I took the back streets, staying off the main roads. I made a turn at Avenue Foch and took in the sights of the city, trying to figure out how to bring my adrenaline down. It always took too long, and I certainly didn't like taking sleeping pills. They made me too groggy. And then there were the nightmares that I couldn't wake up from.

After I made the turn on Avenue Foch, I took a sharp left down one of the quieter streets and headed out of the city. Maybe if I could just get a drive in, open the car up a little, I'd feel more like myself.

I took the next right and drove without much thought to where I was going. It was early fall, so there was a nip in the air. I rolled down the window, letting the chill cool my body. I made a left and a right, getting onto the expressway, and then took an exit I wasn't familiar with.

It led to a suburb, which surprised me. I knew I would definitely need my GPS heading back to the hotel.

I frowned as I came along a deserted tree-covered road between two neighborhoods. The quiet solitude should have calmed me, but instead, my adrenaline spiked. A dewy mist rolled along the edges of the trees, giving them an eerie quality, making my hair stand on end.

Jesus Christ, Kannon, get it together. Nothing was urgent. I didn't need to focus on anything. There were no bad guys tonight, and I could deal with that.

The road curved to the left, and that's when I saw headlights up ahead. They illuminated the road, but they weren't coming *from* the road. I approached slowly and then parked about fifty feet from where I saw the headlights.

The car had slid into a ditch. *Fucking hell.* I parked and then ran around to the back of my car to grab a rope and my rappelling equipment.

Not knowing how far down the driver was, the equipment might come in handy.

I ran to the edge of the road. "Hello? Anyone down there?"

There was a soft voice. "Yes, over here."

A woman. God. My heart hammered in my chest, and I clenched my teeth. *Calm down. It isn't Phoebe.* What the fuck was the woman doing out here? Was she drunk? How did she fall in here?

You can ask questions when you get her out.

At the broken guard rail, I attached the grappling hook before knotting the rope around my waist. Then I eased down into the ditch. It was steep. Climbable if you had the right shoes, but mine were slippery, so the rope would help us climb back up if needed. And if I had to secure her, it would definitely come in handy.

"I'm coming down."

"It's rocky. Be careful."

When I reached the car, it was on the one flat spot of the steep embankment. There were some grassy patches, but the incline wasn't easy.

A woman was leaning out of the passenger side of the car. "You didn't have to come down here. You could have just called the police."

"You want me to go back up? I can leave you if you want," I muttered sardonically. Who declined help when they were in a ditch?

I couldn't see her that well, but I could sense the frown in her tone. "Oh, an American, fantastic. Aren't you hilarious?"

She had an accent. I wasn't sure what. It sounded vaguely British, but I couldn't be sure. "What's your name?"

"I'm London."

"What? Like the city?"

"Oh my God, you have all the original lines."

This was going fucking fantastic. "Well, I guess I'm lucky you didn't meet me in a bar then. I'd be bombing."

"Yes. Yes, you would," she said with a chuckle.

"I don't know about that," I said as I edged over to her, testing the strength of the rope so we wouldn't slide farther down the ravine. "You haven't really seen what I look like yet. My face is hard to turn away from." I didn't know why I was saying these things, but hell, if it helped her not panic, I'd keep going.

"Oh, lucky me, you're modest too."

"Well, you are lucky. I am here to save you."

She licked her lips. "And if I don't need saving?"

I chuckled. "Of course, you don't need saving. You're just down in a ravine, with the possibility of sliding down even farther. Plus, it's rocky and practically impossible to climb without a rope. But you're *fine*."

"I'll have you know I *am* fine. If I hadn't twisted my stupid ankle, I would be out of this ravine already."

I frowned then. "You're hurt?"

"Mostly bumps and bruises. I don't think anything is broken, but my ankle hurts a little. I don't think it's a proper sprain. It's just twisted."

When I reached her side, I could see her better in the moonlight. She did have some cuts and bruises. I knelt in front of her. "I'm Kannon. Kannon Adams."

"Oh, names again? You know mine."

"Well, at least I'm not going to offer to buy you a drink—yet. But from the looks of it, you could probably use one."

"You'd be right. Of course this would happen on a night like tonight."

I assessed her foot. Slim. Delicate. Well arched. A dancer's foot. Except, they were too smooth for her to be a dancer. I lifted her ankle and found it was mildly swollen.

She winced. "Careful."

"Easy does it." When I looked up, her gaze on me was intent. Her blue eyes bore into mine, and that kicked my heart rate up even higher.

What the fuck?

Her hair was in a tangled mess around her face, spilling onto her shoulders. I had to focus to ask her the necessary questions. "Okay, London, how did you get down here?"

She swallowed hard. "I think some idiot ran me off the road."

My brows snapped down, senses going on alert. "What do you mean, *ran you off the road?*"

"I was driving on my way to a friend's house, and out of nowhere, a car came up and banged into the back of my car. I started to pull over to exchange details, but instead, it came around the side of me, sped up, and hit me again. I lost control. And here I am. Then you came along."

Jesus Christ. "I'm sorry."

"Me too. I do hate to be late."

"Hot date?"

"I mean, not as hot as my current situation, but sure."

I grinned at that. She still had a sense of humor. That was good. And I liked her accent. Her voice rolled over me like a nice shot of scotch, warm and smoky. It made me think of doing dirty things to her, making her light up like fire.

Stop it. She clearly needs help. Fantasizing about her was definitely not the best idea at the moment. "I'm going to take your hand. Put as little pressure on your ankle as possible. I'm going to tie you to me, and then I'm going to climb us out of here, okay?"

"How are you going to do that?"

"We're going to climb up. Mostly me. You're going to climb up onto my back and stay there. But you'll still be attached to me, even if you fall off."

"What if I fall? Will you fall too?"

I shook my head. "The grappling hook will hold our weight. You're just a little thing. And it held my weight coming down, so we'll be fine climbing back up."

"Dare I ask why you have a grappling hook?"

"For situations like this."

"Oh my God, you're a serial killer, right? But I'm an easy target. It'll be much better for you if you hunt your prey. And, as I can't run on this ankle, I make a terrible serial killer target."

My lips twitched. "Sweetheart, if I wanted to hurt you, you'd be dead already."

She blinked at me before deadpanning, "That's not as comforting as you think it is."

I shook my head. "Come on. Do you have everything you need?"

She had a sturdy cross-body bag strapped on. It was bulky though. Like a camera bag.

"I couldn't get out of the driver's side, so I shimmied over here. I just need this bag. I've got my phone in here. I have a few things in the back, but they're not urgent. I didn't want to attempt climbing in there and have the car fall farther down."

"Smart girl. You're sure that bag is urgent?"

Her nod was insistent. "I'd probably give my life to secure it."

I lifted a brow but didn't question her. I'd find out soon enough what was in there. "Come on, let's get you out of here."

"Kannon, that's an interesting name. I don't think I've ever met a Kannon."

"Well, not everyone can be as handsome and unique as I am."

"Are you flirting? That sounded like flirting. *Bad* flirting."

I ignored that, not sure what I would say in reply. Instead, I focused on the task at hand. It was easy enough for me to do simple knots and loops around us. The scent of her perfume, the light floral base with spicy accents was a distraction I couldn't afford though.

Then she climbed onto my back. She was light. But that wasn't what I noticed the most. It was her scent again. Something flowery and light with a hint of vanilla? Jasmine? It clouded my brain for just a moment.

Her voice was soft in my ear. "Like this?"

I cleared my throat. "Like that. Hold on tight."

"Are you sure you can hold me?"

I angled my head so our gazes met for a moment. "You don't think I'm strong enough?"

Her lids lowered for a moment, and then she met my gaze. In the moonlight, her skin looked incandescent despite the cuts and bruises. "You're clearly solid enough. I just... I don't want to be too much."

"Miss London, I don't think you are ever too much."

She laughed then. "In that case, I don't think you've met my brothers. They would disagree."

"Well, maybe we'll get you home and I can meet them."

She said nothing in response. I credited that to nerves or

the fact that I didn't make much sense. And then I began our climb up. Without gloves, it was murder on my hands, but I was careful. Choosing which rocks to trust and which ones to avoid. When I lost my footing once, London held on tight, spider monkey style, and squeaked. She had a strong grip.

She didn't panic or scream, which was beyond helpful. When we reached the top, we lay there panting for several moments.

"Oh my God, I honestly thought I was going to die down there. I'd been screaming, but no one heard me. I guess it was all in my head."

"Well, you have so much more life to live. Don't die on my account."

She reached her arms around me and squeezed me tightly. "This doesn't mean I'm a fan of your pickup lines. I'm just really grateful."

Her warm, soft body was pressed up against me, and I didn't know what to do with my hands. Gently, I used one to pat her back until she released me. I eased us apart as much as the rope allowed. "Let's get this rigging off you."

When I had the rope off of the two of us and the grappling hook disconnected, I grabbed my supplies and helped her stand. "Okay, put your arm around my shoulders, and I'll walk you to the car. We'll get you to a hospital so you can get checked out."

"Oh, I don't need a hospital. I just want to get to my friend's place."

I glanced down at her, caught off guard by her tone. "Are you in some kind of trouble?"

She frowned. "No, I just want to get to my friend's. I'm fine."

"These cuts need to be cleaned up, and you are going to bruise come the morning. You're going to look like Barney's cousin."

She lifted a brow. "Who's Barney?"

I sighed. "Giant eggplant-colored dinosaur."

Her lips quirked. "I'm going to look like a dick?"

The laugh tore out of my throat before I realized what I was doing. "Jesus."

She snorted a laugh. "Yes, I know who Barney is."

"You're fucking with me?"

"A little."

I sighed. "God, save me from sarcastic women."

She gave a prim shake of her head. "I can do this all day."

She probably could. I wasn't going to let her do that though. "Let's get you in the passenger seat, Captain America. We can argue about where I'm taking you once we're settled in."

"Nice movie reference. I like how you slid that right in. As far as where we're going, you're taking me to my friend's house."

I rolled my eyes. "Uh-huh. Feet in. Careful of the ankle."

She winced a little, but then she sat back and practically moaned as she sank into the leather. "Oh my God, this leather is divine."

"I know, right? Seats might be the sole reason I bought this car."

I closed the door, deposited my tools and her bag in the trunk, and then climbed into the driver's seat. "Okay, I still say we need to take you to a hospital. At the very least, we should call the police."

"And I will call them. I swear. I mostly just really want a hot soak."

"You could have internal injuries."

She met my gaze stubbornly. "I'll call a doctor to come to the house."

My brows lifted then. "A doctor to come to the house?"

"You know, like a concierge service. This is Paris; I know they have them. And I guarantee you, Rian will have the name of one."

Well, she was rich then. Filthy, stinking rich. My favorite kind of client.

Except she's not a client. And she smells like sin and temptation.

No, she wasn't a client. She was a beautiful woman who was clearly hurt and needed a doctor at a hospital.

However, it looked like I would have to give in to her wishes. "All right, which way is your friend's place? I'll take you there, speak to her, make sure she gets you a doctor, and then I'm out of here."

"Just when we were getting along so well."

"Well, it doesn't seem that my lines are working on you, so I feel like I struck out."

"God, man. Be persistent."

Despite the seriousness of the situation, I wanted to smile again. She was gorgeous with all that midnight-dark hair. And those startling eyes had a way of grabbing a man...where it counted. "Oh, I'm persistent." I slid my gaze over her, and I wanted to smack myself.

Focus, Kannon, she's hurt. That fact didn't stop me from recognizing that she was also gorgeous, but I knew that was mostly the adrenaline talking. *Fight. Flight. Or fuck.* And at the moment, we were solidly in fuck territory. It didn't help that her pouty mouth kept taunting me.

I cleared my throat and turned my attention to the road as I started my engine.

Her voice was soft next to me. "Kannon, thank you."

"You're welcome, London. I still think it's an odd name."

"Well, what kind of name is Kannon anyway? Let me guess, you spell it fancy with a K instead of a C?"

I coughed a laugh. "You sure are right."

"Of course, I am."

We were still laughing when the bright headlights of a car joined us on the road.

"Well, the good news is, someone else would have come along eventually." I angled my head toward the headlights. "You can rest assured that you wouldn't have ended up alone there all night."

"This is me, resting assured."

She glanced back at the car as I eased out onto the road. I cleared my throat. "What are you going to do with your friend?"

Her voice was distant, distracted as she glanced back. "Mostly lay low and catch up. I haven't seen her for a bit."

I couldn't help but laugh. "You're telling me, you came all the way to Paris during Fashion Week and you're not going to catch a show?"

"Nope. It might surprise you to know that I happen to like quiet and subdued."

Something about her diamond stud earrings and the Diamonds by the Yard wrapped around her wrist told me that was inaccurate. But hell, her plans didn't matter to me.

Except there was something in her tone. Something that told me there was more to what she was saying. Something my curiosity wouldn't let die. "And what do you do?"

There was a bit of hesitation before she said, "I'm a photographer. Sometimes a photojournalist."

I glanced over to her. Her tone said it wasn't exactly a lie, but there was something she was leaving out about her job.

None of your business. Just take her to wherever she's going and be done with her.

The headlights were coming up on us quickly, and I frowned. I increased my speed a little, but the other car didn't fall back. They only increased their speed to match.

I glanced at her. "London?"

She turned her head. "Hm? Yes, Kannon?"

"How much trouble are you in?"

Her eyes went wide. "What do you mean?"

"That car, it's following us." I slowed my pace, and it lunged forward. "And what are the chances that the car that ran you off the road earlier only did it by accident?"

She shook her head. "There's no reason anyone would want to run me off the road. It was just a hit and run."

And then I heard it...the ping off my rear bumper. The car lurched forward. London didn't scream, but she immediately ducked and cowered. "Oh fuck."

That fight or flight impulse went immediately to fight. "London, I need you to reach into the glove compartment and get my gun for me."

"What the fuck? Why do you have a gun?"

"Because I run a security company. My car is bullet-proof, but someone is shooting at us."

Another *ping*. She ducked again, and I swerved. The car could take several hits, but the tires...the tires weren't bulletproof. We'd be incapacitated and sitting ducks if they hit one of them.

Another *ping*.

And then another car appeared out from behind the one that was following us.

Fuck me. "They've got a friend."

That car veered around to the side. A shooter was aiming at my car and fired, but nothing.

"London, stay down right there where you are. Hand me my gun."

She reached into the glove compartment and handed it to me, her hands quick as if she'd handled one before but wasn't a fan of them. "What are you going to do?"

"Generally when someone shoots at you, you shoot back."

"What? What in the world?"

With my gun in my palm and a couple of taps of the buttons, my seat leaned back just enough that I was out of the direct line of fire, and I hit one of the special modification buttons I'd put into the car, forcibly dropping the windows. They slid down, and I aimed and fired into the other car. It swerved and careened, but the driver was unable to control the vehicle because he was very, very dead. The car tumbled and rolled and pitched into the line of trees with a loud crash and plenty of smoke.

London stared at me. "What the hell?"

"Stay down. We still have another one to deal with."

The other car swerved, coming up to our side.

I hit the button again, rolling the windows up, and then we were jostled with a loud scraping bang. *My fucking car.*

This time, London did scream. "Kannon!"

"Try to stay calm and breathe, in through your nose, out through your mouth, and count your breaths."

"What? You're trying to be a Zen master when people are shooting at us?"

Another *bang,* and I held on to the wheel tightly. "Down, love."

"I'm not your—"

I reached over and shoved her head down. With my free hand, I hit the button, turned around, and then fired. Two pops, easily. *Crack. Crack.* The first one missed, the second one hit part of the wheels at least, because the car screeched and careened. The driver was fighting for the wheel. I immediately slammed on the brakes, screeched us around, and aimed for the car.

I threw the BMW into park, and London screamed, "What the hell are you doing?"

"I'm going to ask him some questions."

"He has a gun."

I held up my hand. "So do I. Stay here and stay down."

"What if something happens to you?"

"If something happens to me that means that motherfucker in there is a professional. And you are dead anyway."

That was me, the caretaker that soothed nerves.

Gun in hand, I slowly approached the other car. I reached the driver's side. The window was shattered, and the driver was gasping for breath. White male. Dark hair. Dark eyes. "Who are you? Why are you shooting at us?"

He spat. "Fuck you."

He had an accent similar to hers. British, but grittier. South London, maybe? "Talk."

"And I said, fuck you."

"Okay, we can do this the hard way." I bent to open the door, but he hit the gas, tires screeching as he peeled off. I recognized why he didn't shoot me then. His gun had fallen out of his hand and he couldn't reach it.

I scowled as I watched the car become smaller and smaller on the road. I jogged back to my vehicle. "Okay, he's gone. Do you want to tell me who he is? Do you

CARRIE ANN RYAN & NANA MALONE

want to tell me why some British tossers are after you?"
London didn't answer though. "London?"

My heart rate kicked up. *No. No. No. No.* I reached
for her. She still had a pulse. Then I grabbed my pen
light from the console. I checked her eyes. Christ, she'd
passed out. It was highly likely she had a concussion.

You should have checked for that before, you idiot.

Fuck. There would be no getting her to her friend's.
There would be no getting answers tonight. I didn't
really have many options She was hurt, and those idiots
who were just shooting at us might come back. I had no
choice but to take her with me. Whoever she was,
clearly, she needed help. No way was I leaving her here.

Chapter 5
LONDON

One room. One bed. One major problem.

BRIGHT LIGHTS SHONE BEHIND MY EYELIDS, AND I groaned, refusing to open my eyes and face the truth. Whatever that may be. Because if I opened my eyes and remembered what had happened the day or night or week before, then I'd have to deal with it. And frankly, I wasn't sure if I wanted to.

"Good, you're awake."

I groaned again as I forced myself to open my eyes, the blinding light hitting my retinas so fiercely that I lowered my lids again and turned over, trying not to vomit.

"What happened?"

"Come on, let me see your face."

The growly voice seemed far too loud for whatever room we were in. I knew it was male, but I had no idea who the hell it belonged to. To make matters worse I didn't know where I was to begin with.

That probably should've caused a bit of concern, but for the moment, I just needed my head to stop pounding and for whoever was growling to move away.

"London, open your damn eyes." The tone was sharp.

That forced my eyes open quickly. I immediately narrowed them at the man in front of me. He had tousled blond hair, striking blue eyes, and a chiseled jaw covered in a few-days-old beard that pegged him as a long-lost Hemsworth brother. His gaze narrowed in a match to mine.

"You don't need to shout," I snapped as I tried to lever myself up. I moved far too quickly, though, because nausea swept over me, and my stomach pitched. I would have moaned if I hadn't thought I'd embarrass myself and vomit.

"Feel better, London?" he asked, the sarcasm in his tone making me want to punch him. Slowly, my memories returned in a scrapbook patchwork of the night before. I remembered just who I was looking at now.

For starters, he was far better-looking than my hazy

memory gave him credit for. Either that or I had some sort of concussion and my vision couldn't be trusted. But I remembered the way he'd hooked me to his back last night then climbed us out of the ravine. I remembered the rock-hard feel of his muscles. And God, his damn smell.

And worse, I remembered wanting to nuzzle into it.

Given the memory of just how strong he was, I'd likely hurt myself if I hit him. I opened my eyes again and assessed the man sitting next to me on the tiny bed. He was built, broad and tall, given how far his legs extended. His thick muscle was more than apparent under his relaxed-fit long-sleeve T-shirt. I had basically been rescued by Thor. *Excellent.*

The fact that my mouth watered had nothing to do with the head injury I'd sustained the night before. He was...stunning. I would never admit it, but drooling was definitely a possibility.

"Why are you on my bed?"

He snorted. "It's *our* bed, baby. You'd better get accustomed to sharing."

I ran the word *our* through my head. Then blinked. Had he slept next to me? "Excuse me?" I asked, looking around and groaning again at the pain in my head.

"I need to check you for a concussion." With strong fingers, he lifted my chin and shined a light into my eyes.

My world spun, and nausea rose as my mind replayed everything that had happened. I needed to focus. I forced a deep breath, trying to regain some of my meager control. I hated feeling like I couldn't grasp hold of my life. Like I was spinning and there was nothing I could do to fix it.

Focus, London. "What happened?"

"You don't remember?" He mumbled a few things to himself that I couldn't understand but nodded as he looked at me. As if checking out my eyes had reaffirmed any previous diagnosis he had made when I was passed out.

"No, of course I remember what happened last night. I just don't understand how I ended up in bed. With you."

His smirk was slow but held a note of worry. "You passed out after we got shot at. I didn't have any other choice, so I brought you here. This is my hotel room. Looks like you'll be fine though."

His hotel room? Hell. And why did he sound vaguely annoyed by the idea?

"How do you know I'm fine?"

"Because I checked you over. Your ankle is a little swollen. You may have a slight concussion and definitely some bumps and bruises, but you're no worse for wear. Nothing broken. Nothing that indicates internal bleeding. I'd like to have a doctor look you over though."

The violation slid over me like an oil slick, and I pushed at him.

"How did you manage that while I was passed out?" I asked, my voice going into a higher octave with each word.

"Nothing like that. Jesus Christ." He calmly pushed to his feet as if to give me space. "I had to do a quick check before I moved you from the roadside to here. I didn't want to do any more damage than necessary." He also slowed the cadence of his voice to something level and calming. Like he was used to dealing with hysterical people. "Every other room in the hotel and the surrounding hotels is booked. The room my company booked for me is it. It's one nobody can trace, but there's only one bed. I would have put you with my associate, Sparrow, but her room is tiny and only has a twin and I figured someone should watch you. I put you to bed after I made sure you were okay. And you are. You're going to be fine."

"I don't understand." Even trying to think about what had happened last night sent the hairs on my arms to attention.

He eased into the chair near the foot of the bed. "I gather you're confused. And I know this scenario has to be stressful. I'm only here to help."

He was doing it again. The gravel in his voice more of a low purr than actual words. "You don't have to talk to me like that. I'm not a child. And I'm not going to bolt or do anything stupid." I raised my chin, something I had learned to do at a young age. I'd had to learn the art of showing disdain and yet looking regal at the same time early on.

I hated that look. Aunt Rebecca had taught it to me long ago. Sometimes it was the only way to get rid of people who saw too much or wanted too much. She'd been the only one I could rely on when I lost my parents, and I did my best to remember what she'd taught me.

"I don't think you are. We don't know who was out there chasing you, and we're in fucking France, not your home or mine. So while we figure out what the hell we're going to do, you're going to stay here in my room, the one place where I can keep you safe."

"Who are you?" I asked, wondering how the hell I had ended up in this situation.

I'd left home wanting room to breathe. None of this was anything I had bargained for. I just needed time for my brothers to work out how to fix this arcane rule. I had to believe they would because I wasn't about to open my uterus for business, no matter what. Children should be brought into the world for love, not necessity or a crown.

For now I needed to stay off everybody's radar. Kannon had done the right thing. He'd protected me. Kept me safe.

Jesus Christ, I had been shot at. Just the memory made my heart race, and I pressed my palm over my chest, trying to calm the rising panic. I was safe for now and needed to think. I had more important things to worry about.

Namely, how the hell I was going to get out of this situation and who Kannon was exactly.

Could I trust him? He'd kept me safe for the night. I hoped to hell I could put my faith in him, but hell, besides his name, I knew nothing about the man. I didn't even know his last name.

"I'm a security specialist. A consultant."

I frowned. "Vague terminology for someone who knows how to handle a gun."

"It's my job to protect people. I'm here for Paris Fashion Week," he said. "I ran into you when I closed out that job."

"I'm grateful you did." I whispered the words.

His brow furrowed. "Were you here for the shows? Who knew you were going to be here?"

"I—no one. Just Rian. My family. I wasn't really here for the shows."

"Not one show? It's the hottest ticket in Paris."

"I know, but we just wanted girl time."

He lifted a brow that told me he didn't exactly believe me. "Girl time. Right. What is it you do, London?"

I frowned at him. What was with this tone? He sounded suspicious. Worse, he sounded like Wilder. That calm countenance. The simple question then the quiet calm as he waited for a response. It was infuriating.

I'd once asked Wilder why he did that. And he'd told me that the quieter you were, the more suspicious people tended to talk. Their own discomfort made them eager to spill. Just what the hell did Kannon suspect me of?

I was done with that tone. He might have saved my life, but I didn't know him, and I didn't need to tell him my life story. "It's none of your business."

"I got shot at with you in my car. That makes it my business."

"I didn't ask you to protect me."

"Well, it seems like I'm going to be protecting you anyway, princess."

"My name is London," I gritted out. "Call me London."

"Shouldn't I call you Princess London?"

I lifted my chin. "You know who I am."

"Of course, I know who you are. Your face is splashed on all the tabloids. Last night I wasn't certain. But in the clear morning light, I knew exactly who was in my bed, Goldilocks. You're even more famous than the London royals." His smirk made his eyes go smoky, not that I noticed. "Nice coincidence on the name."

I flipped him off. He'd already made fun of my name twice now. He didn't get a third chance.

"Hey, that's not what a princess should do. Is that your royal finger?"

"Okay, I'm done. I need to go. I need to make sure everyone knows that I'm safe."

"We can make that happen."

"You keep saying 'we.' Who do you mean by *we*?"

"My team. I sent Sparrow and Olly to look at the site from last night. We don't know who was shooting at you, but it looked like a professional job. So you're not safe. We're going to make sure you're safe. *I'm* going to make sure you're safe."

"Sure. While you do whatever it is you do, I need to contact my brothers."

"We will. But first, you're going to give me your phone."

My gaze widened, tension crawling up my spine. "Okay, now this sounds like you're taking it. Once you have it, what's to stop you from just abducting me? You can't have my phone. You can't have anything. I'm going home."

Home, where apparently, I was supposed to marry a duke and have babies and never have a choice in my life.

That option sounded better than being dead, sure,

but there had to be a third option. One where I wasn't in a room with a man who was prowling around me like a caged lion. One where I wasn't hurt because I'd been shot at and run off the road.

I scrambled off the bed, this time with Kannon letting me do so.

"I need to call my brothers."

"We've got that handled. And I'm sorry, but you need to give me your phone."

I whirled on him. "Why? So you can call for ransom?"

He gave me a beleaguered sigh. "No, so we can make sure that nobody can trace where you are."

"What the hell are you talking about?"

"I've been taking care of business like this for a long time. In cases like these, people like this, they don't give up. They'll be back. Which means they feel confident in their ability to find you again. And the easiest way to find someone is to track their phone."

"And I've dealt with security professionals before. For my entire life, actually. So no, I'm going to call my family, and *they're* going to take care of me."

His sharp blue gaze narrowed. "You like that? People taking care of you?"

"You're trying to do the same thing to me!"

"Maybe, but it's my job."

"I didn't hire you." I was yelling now. I didn't want to yell, but my panic was rising.

"No, you didn't. But me getting shot at? That kind of puts me on the job no matter what. And I'm more than a little pissed off that someone took shots at me. I'm not a fan of someone trying to take a piece out of my ass. Like it or not, I'm going to figure out who shot at you, and you're just going to have to deal with it." His voice rose to match mine.

"Stop yelling at me!"

"You're yelling right back, princess."

"You don't talk to me like that."

"What are you going to do about it, *princess*?"

"I'm going to leave. I'll take my chances. Worse comes to worst, I'll go back to the airport and go home."

"If you do that, someone's going to find you, and they're going to shoot you. Just like they tried to last night."

"Don't you try and scare me. I'm already there. It can't get worse. What do I have to lose?"

"I'm not trying to scare you, princess. I'm just telling you the truth."

"Stop calling me princess."

"It's what you are. A precious little protected princess who's never seen the real world. And suddenly someone's shooting at you. I get it. It comes with the job. Well, my job is to make sure that doesn't happen again.

Now, give me your damn phone so I can make sure they can't find you. And *then* we're going to call your brothers and see what they want."

Un-fucking-believable. "And what about what *I* want?"

"You want to stay alive? Then give me your phone."

He pushed to his feet and loomed over me. I could feel the waves of heat emanating from his body. What the hell? It was just the adrenaline spiking through me, the confusion of everything.

I was not attracted to this man. He was a caveman. A bossy one at that.

But someone had shot at me, and someone had known where I was and tried to kill me. He wasn't wrong. *You need to trust him.*

Bile filled my throat, my hands started to shake, and I cursed at myself. I was just hungry. It was just a blood sugar issue. That was it. I refused to let fear take over.

Kannon gave me a pitying look, and I wanted to hit him again. I wanted to scream and to thrash and to just make everything go away. Because I didn't have control here, and that was the one thing I'd strived for all of my life. The control to do something. But every time I turned around, someone kept stripping it away from me.

"Let me help you with this, and we'll get you home. Then you never have to see me again."

I didn't really have any other choice. "Fine."

"You can relax. I'm not going to hurt you. Right now, I'm whoever you need me to be." And with that line, he moved past me, riffled through my purse, and pulled out my phone. I wanted to throw something. I wanted to say something. But instead, I just stood there, my hands fisted at my sides, glaring at him.

"You're taking a lot of liberties."

"I'm trying to save your life." He turned away to look down at his phone as if I hadn't spoken. *Jerk.* "We'll contact your brothers, and we'll see what they say."

"And I don't have a choice?"

"When it comes to your safety? No, not really."

I hadn't felt safe in a long while, and the last twenty-four hours were just one more step into that inevitable cage that was my royal throne.

Chapter 6
KANNON

This is going to be a problem.
Scratch that.
She's going to be a problem.

WALKING AWAY HAD BEEN FOR THE BEST, OR I would have turned that princess over my knee.

Fury surged through me, but I did my best not to pay attention to it as I looked down at London's phone. *Lock it down. Every emotion. Tuck it away.*

I was good at that. There was no need for me to let emotions influence what I needed to do. Alden's Princess might not have hired me for this job, but I'd be damned if I let anyone else down on my watch.

I knew she was scared. But she didn't understand. If I wavered for even a moment, she could get hurt or worse.

Memories of screams echoed in my head, a woman calling my name. I dug my hands into the sides of my head, trying to push those images and sounds out of my mind. There was no use dwelling on them.

I wasn't that person anymore.

Also, fuck those memories.

I needed to deal with the London situation, and then I'd be back to even. She was right; she wasn't a client. I'd do the minimum to make her someone else's problem and walk away. Get her to safety. That was all.

I had Olly and Sparrow at my disposal. Olly was still dealing with scrubbing Lilith from any footage. *You want to call Sparrow for what? To talk? Bullshit.*

She'd worry about me and wonder what the hell I was doing.

Somehow, in a business where we were supposed to be about security and taking care of other people, I had a mother hen on my team. What was worse was if she sensed I was having any residual memories; she'd call the whole team back to Paris. And I didn't need them all clucking.

I groaned before I made my way back to the bedroom. *Our* bedroom.

Fuck. Nope. Just the room that was available.

CARRIE ANN RYAN & NANA MALONE

It hadn't even crossed my mind to put London in any other room but mine. It didn't matter that I could have put her in Sparrow's or found a way to keep her out of my bed. But as soon as she had winked at me the night before, if I was honest with myself, all I had wanted to do was make sure that she was in my sights at all times.

The problem was, I liked her. She had a quick, sharp wit and she'd managed to make me laugh last night... before all the bullets.

As if I had time for that kind of bullshit. She was in my bed, but I sure fucking wasn't.

There was no way I was going down that road.

She was a princess, and I was just a guy who had shown up in the right place at the wrong time. I hadn't even been hired to keep her safe, but I'd be damned if I let her get hurt. I'd get her pert little ass home, then I'd be done.

Then deal with her.

I knew that twisting feeling in my gut. The one that kept me in the suite's living area... It was fear. I was losing my goddamn mind.

Sac up. She's a princess. She can't hurt you.

Lies. But still, I went back into the room and pierced her with a grim, determined expression. In response, she scowled back. She had her arms wrapped around her knees, and it looked like she was counting to herself, probably to hold back that temper. How often did she do that? I had to admit that I liked it when she spit fire though.

Because even though I knew that she had that fear within her, she still had a temper on her and wasn't afraid to match me. And if I was capable of caring about another human being like that, I probably would have thought it was hot.

But no way.

"Okay, we're calling your brothers." I held up the device I'd retrieved from the other room. "This device will scramble our location. But you still need to be brief. Do you understand?"

She nodded enthusiastically and scrambled off the bed, and I reached out to steady her as she tilted to the side. I was worried about that. She should be steadier, shouldn't she? Max was the one on my team with the real medical training, and I wondered if I should give him a call.

She was warm to the touch, and she pulled away as if I had shocked her. And maybe I had. Perhaps it was just static electricity and not whatever the fuck else was going on between us.

Because there sure as hell wasn't *anything* going on between us.

She let out a breath, probably annoyed with herself for moving too fast after getting hurt, but then she was all regal business again. "Is this phone safe? Because you seem to think mine isn't."

"Your phone *might* be safe, but why risk it? Between using this sat phone and the IP relay, this should be safe."

She stared at me, unblinking, before shaking her head. "Whatever. I'm calling my brothers. We're going to end this."

"Sounds like a plan, princess."

"Stop it," she whispered while dialing numbers on the phone.

I was surprised she knew any of their numbers. Most people these days didn't know phone numbers off the top of their heads. But then I realized most royals knew to memorize specific numbers to get where they needed to go.

I was surprised she hadn't had a panic button on her.

Maybe she had and just hadn't pressed it.

I didn't know much about her, only what the tabloids told me and what little she'd told me about herself.

I was intrigued by her. That fierce personality and the way she'd told me that she was a photojournalist with such passion and excitement. Maybe I could have believed it if I hadn't seen her face on a tabloid in a supermarket stand.

She was beauty personified, sex with curves and pouty lips.

And I refused to even let my mind go further down that path.

"Roman."

She only said her brother's name, the King of Alden, before she held the phone back, a deep grumble of a voice shouting back at her.

"Are you done?" she asked and then pulled the phone away again.

I stalked over to her and tore the cell from her hand.

She reached for it, but I held it up above her head. And when she jumped, pressing her body against mine, we both froze for a minute. And then she took a staggering step back. I ignored the ache, or whatever the hell I was feeling, and put the phone to my ear. "Stop yelling at your sister, or I'm going to hang up."

"Who the fuck are you?"

"I'm the man who contacted you last night," I said, and I could practically feel the daggers from London.

"Kannon?" Roman asked, anger in his cultured voice.

"That's me. And here's your sister back. We're going to put you on speakerphone. Don't fucking yell at her."

"I'm her king, you asshat."

"And I don't give a flying fuck." I put the phone on speaker and laid it on the bed between us.

CARRIE ANN RYAN & NANA MALONE

London just blinked at me before her cheeks went red and she picked up the phone. She didn't, however, turn off the speaker.

"You knew? They called you?"

"Of course, they called me. You were run off the road? Jesus Christ, London. I'm sending men to you right now."

"The accident was just a one-off thing. And for all I know, the shooters who came later could have been after Kannon."

I didn't know if she actually believed the lie or if she was just trying to make sure her brother didn't worry.

"They weren't," I said. I had already cleaned up the messes that would have come after me. There was enough blood on my hands that nobody needed to worry.

"We already looked up Kannon Security. They're likely who we would have called in that situation if we couldn't bring our own people," the king said, surprising me.

Maybe I would like her brother. Not that it mattered.

"I'm fine. I just don't know why any of this happened."

"We're going to figure it out," Roman soothed. "But the reason you left is still an issue here. I'm working with the council, but I'm getting pushback. If you show up right now, it's going to be an issue, and I'm not going to be able to get us out of it." He paused, and I looked at London, wondering what the hell the king was talking about.

"London, if you came home, I'd never force you into that situation, but it's going to take away our options."

"What are you saying?" she asked, and I wanted to reach out. I wanted to tell her everything would be okay. Because I knew she was so damn strong, and yet she looked nothing of the sort standing there in front of me at the moment.

"I'm saying I'll send my people to get you if that's what you want, but Wilder gives a thumbs-up on Kannon. He's been vetting him while we've been talking. He's good to protect you. As long as he watches his fucking tone."

I ground my teeth together, but I didn't say anything. I did what I always did; I swallowed what I wanted to say for the greater good. Besides, me shouting just then would probably end up with my neck in a guillotine or some royal shit.

"You can't just hire random people. I'm fine. I just need to get to Rian."

"Do you honestly think going to your vapid actress friend can keep you safe? You're going to put Rian in the middle of everything and endanger her. She's likely to drag you to a party and expose you."

"First off, Rian is so much more than a 'vapid actress' as you called her. You know that. I don't know what you have against her." She held up a hand as I opened my mouth to say they were getting off the subject, but she shook her head. "That has nothing to do with this, other than you're an asshole."

"I am, but that isn't new."

"I don't want to put her in danger, and I won't. When she rescheduled her flight, she told me to head out to her place in the country. You remember she had a stalker five years ago? This house is where she hid out. It comes complete with a panic room."

As her brother railed about how he didn't know the specs of said panic room, London bit her lip and started to pace the room, though the space wasn't all that big for her to move around. Every time she went past me, her arm brushed against mine, and I bit back a groan.

Focus, man. Lock it down.

I did not want this need, this urge to put my hands on her and tell her everything was going to be okay. Besides, I knew better. I knew what happened when someone slipped by my carefully constructed defenses.

And I wasn't that man anymore. I was a liar. I had lied the last time I told someone everything would be fine and that we'd make it out alive.

I had lied, and she had burned, taking every good part of me with her. I'd relearned those hard lessons.

Focused on what I could control. On what was ahead of me. Emotion clouded the mind and ripped out the heart.

I wouldn't be that man again.

"I need to be able to handle myself, Roman," London said, and I could practically hear the plea in her voice. Maybe not to her brother but begging for herself.

"I know that, London. But we both knew your freedom of movement was going to be a problem. Especially when it seems that someone wants to hurt you."

"It just doesn't make any sense," she whispered.

"I know, but we're going to find out who's behind this. You know Breck and Wilder are already on it."

She ran her hands through her dark chocolatey hair. "Maybe it's mistaken identity. That's possible, right? I've done nothing to warrant someone trying to kill me. Fair enough if they wanted to kidnap and ransom me, but kill me? Who in the world hates me that much? It has to be some kind of mistake."

"I'm going to assume that anyone shooting at my baby sister wants to hurt *her*. Therefore, if I have to wrap you up in cotton wool and put thirty armed guards around you to protect you, that is what I'm going to do."

"Roman." She pinched the bridge of her nose. "Just... Tell Aunt Rebecca and Kate that I'm okay. That they don't have to worry about me. Lie if you have to, but they don't need the stress."

"I can do that, but London? I've left you on your

tether long enough, and now you've pulled too far. I'm going to officially hire Kannon Security to protect you until you can come back home. Listen to him. Do what he says. If you must go to Rian's, then I want Kannon vetting that house. Stay safe."

"Roman," she shouted, turning off the speaker and putting the phone to her ear before running to the bathroom to lock herself in for some semblance of privacy. She whispered so I couldn't hear her, but I knew she was probably ripping her brother a new one.

There was a knock on the door. I looked through the peephole and opened it a crack after seeing it was Sparrow.

"Olly said we might have a job?" she asked.

"Yes, I think we do."

"Okay, we'll get it set up. You need the usual? Fresh clothes, cash, weapons?"

"Yep. I'll work with her and send you the location of where we'll be. I need Olly to work his magic and get me schematics of the place before we arrive."

She searched my gaze, and I wasn't sure she liked what she saw. "Be careful, boss."

"Always am," I said. She just shook her head, and I wanted to curse at her. But I couldn't.

Because we both knew I lied. I wasn't always careful. And sometimes it cost people their lives.

I closed and locked the door after she left and turned as London came out of the bathroom.

"I take it you didn't enjoy the phone call?" I asked, knowing I was an asshole.

She narrowed her gaze. "No, I didn't. But apparently, I don't have a choice in the matter. I don't have a choice in a lot of matters."

"I'm not going to force you into anything, but I am going to keep you safe."

"Because my brother said to?" she asked, folding her arms over her chest. I tried not to look at the way the movement made her breasts lift.

Damn it. "Your other choice is to go home." I spread my hands. "These are your choices. Choose well, princess."

She puffed out a breath. "If I go back to Alden, things are going to get worse for my country, or at least for our family."

"Rian is the woman you were on your way to?"

"Yes. She was supposed to be here this week but got delayed for work. But she was still going to let me stay at her place in the city to get away for a while."

My attention locked on what she said. "Get away from who?"

She shook her head. "I don't think that what I'm running from at the moment has anything to do with who could be after me. *If* there is anyone after me."

This was the thing with wealthy clients. Nothing was ever as it seemed. "Hold up here. Let's just assume for the moment that someone *is* after you, because your pretending that you didn't get shot at is just idiotic."

"Please don't do that. I get enough patronizing shit from my family. I'm not pretending anything. I know of no reason anyone would want me dead. So being of sound, rational mind, I don't jump to the immediate conclusion that I, London, was being shot at. No one has anything to gain by me being dead." Her jaw was tight, and her voice clipped as she spoke.

"All I know is that as soon as you got into the car, *after* you'd already been run off the road once, bullets came at me. Bullets came at *both* of us, but no one tried to run *me* off the road. I'm going to assume it was you they were after. We are here to protect you, just like your brother wants."

"And I don't have a say."

"Apparently not. But you're not an idiot."

"You sure are acting like I am."

I ran my hand over my hair and cursed. Feelings. I had to find my feelings and employ empathy. How hard could that be? "I know you're scared. I get it. But you need to tell me what you're on the run from so we can get you home when the threat is neutralized. Your safety is the only thing that matters."

"You believe that?" she asked and shook her head.

"I'm in a cage again, and this time it's not one of my own making." She sighed and turned away from me. "Or maybe it is."

"What are you talking about?" I wanted to reach out to her, but I didn't. There would be no use.

"I'll tell you why I can't go home, but it has nothing to do with who might have shot at us."

"Lay it on me."

"There is an obscure law in our kingdom that states if there is no heir to our generation by the time the youngest of us reaches thirty, the entire family line loses the throne, and it goes to the next in line. In our case, it would be my cousin, Barkley."

I blinked at her, shaking my head. "Excuse me?"

"What I'm saying to you right now is a secret. Nobody else can know. If one of my brothers or I do not produce a child within the year, since I just turned twenty-nine, my brother loses his crown, the family loses its throne completely, and the title goes to my cousin. My Aunt Rebecca is doing everything she can, along with my brothers, to try to fix this, but the Council of Lords wants my brother out."

"I have so many questions," I said, shaking my head. "But first, why does the council want your brother out? For a king, he doesn't seem like a bad guy. I mean he's a bit of an asshole but par for the course, right?"

And I didn't even have to have a tooth pulled or an

arm twisted to say that.

"You guys just yelled at each other and threatened one another," she said, rolling her eyes. "Men."

"He wants you safe. You're his sister. I don't see a problem."

"You wouldn't, would you? And the Council of Lords doesn't like my brother because he's progressive. He doesn't want the roadblocks of tradition and heritage stopping the way of progress and hindering the health of our community and our people. He steps on toes, and he is an arrogant jerk about it. If they can get someone like my philandering drunken cousin on the throne, something they can mold, all the better."

"And you don't think that's a reason for people to shoot at you?"

She shrugged. "Roman's been making waves since he took the throne. At first, he let Aunt Rebecca guide his decisions, but once he started going off book and making his own decisions, many of the council felt threatened. They hated his choice of fiancée. They hate the changes he wants to bring about regarding how laws are handled for commoners. Equal pay. Criminal justice reform. He's vocal. Not just on our local stage either. There are many who would prefer someone else rule."

"Again, enough to kill you?"

She shook her head. "He does have enemies. Some who would look for a way to hurt him. Lord Osterow threatened him publicly about the criminal justice law. Said it would be the end of Roman. Lord Banks threatened to put a measure to vote to limit the royal allowances when Roman pushed through equal pay for women four years ago. He was so angry. He was drunk one night at a ball and told Roman he would ruin him." She sighed. "So now they're trying to use an arcane rule to force me to produce a child. If they truly wanted Roman off the throne, then the Council of Lords would do something to him, not me. I'm fourth in line. And the easiest thing to do is to let me be. No way am I getting married and having a kid in the next year. There is no reason to kill me. None."

I thought it through. Maybe somebody didn't want to wait for the crown. "Are your brothers safe?"

She paled a bit but nodded tightly. "They have security too, even though Roman hates it. They all do. The only reason I didn't was that I've never traveled under my own name, and I was safe. I've done it before."

"Could someone have followed you?"

"No one is trying to kill me," she said softly. There was steel in her voice. Like she *needed* to believe it.

"And what if they are?

"All they want is for me to produce a child."

"With who?" The bitter bile of jealousy ate away at me. No way was I fucking jealous of an imaginary random asshole.

CARRIE ANN RYAN & NANA MALONE

"I'm not." She let out a breath. "My aunt has a farfetched plan to marry me off to some duke. It's the twenty-first century, and I'm still going to be forced into an arranged marriage with a man I don't even like to produce an heir, even though my brothers could do the same exact thing. But no, I'm the woman; therefore, I get to be the one who spreads her legs."

An all-too-ready image of London spreading her legs under me flashed in my head, and my cock twitched.

Jesus Christ. I was losing my damn mind. I needed to sleep. I needed to get her out of my thoughts.

"Okay, then. Let's assume that this could be a reason."

Her brow furrowed. "If that is the case, then I'm worried about my brothers."

"I get that. But like you said, they are well-protected and there is nothing you can do to help them. You are the priority right now."

"Am I? Because if they're coming after me, they could go after them too. Roman is a better target."

"I'll get Sparrow on it. She'll contact their people, and we'll figure it out. You and your family will be safe." I just hoped to hell I wasn't lying like I had the last time.

That scream echoed in my mind again, and I cursed myself.

"I can't believe this is happening," London said.

"But it is, and we can't stay here for long. There are

people after you, and if they knew where to try and run you off the road, then they're watching you. They might have access to cameras and surveillance, so this is just going to be a temporary stop. We're going to need to get you to someplace safer."

"Okay," she said before rolling her shoulders back and looking like the fierce princess I had met the night before. "As long as my brothers are safe, that's all that matters. I'll listen to you. Still, Rian has a safe place for me to go. *If* there's someone actually after me."

"Bullets, London. And we'll see about you going to this Rian's."

"I heard you the first time. I'll go along with this because not doing so would make me an idiot. However, I'm not just going to kneel and do everything you say."

Visions of her kneeling filled my head this time, but I did a better job of hiding my reaction. "You're going to listen, princess. Because I'm the one who's going to keep you alive."

"I'll listen to you because I'm not stupid. But you don't have to act like an asshole."

"Baby, I'm always an asshole." And then I turned on my heel and walked out of the room, needing some air.

Somehow, I was her protector. I was the one who was going to have to keep her alive.

I just had to get her off my fucking mind first.

Chapter 7
LONDON

I thought a bed was for resting.

I'D BEEN IN HERE TOO LONG.

But the scalding-hot water had felt like such a reprieve after the call from hell. I wasn't sure what I expected from Roman. I honestly should have known. He loved me; I knew that. Deep down, deep inside, when I looked really hard, I could see it, but damn, he really thought he was my father and not my brother.

One advantage of the shower was that it washed away the tears and I didn't have to crumble in front of Kannon. He already made me feel unsettled and my skin far too itchy. I wasn't going to add tears to the mix.

To make it all worse, I'd sneakily checked my emails. I knew what Kannon had said. I knew that prolonged usage of the phone and checking email could let someone know where I was. But I needed to check in with work.

Before I left home, I'd emailed my boss Brianne and let her know I had to pass on Brazil due to travel plans.

Travel plans, right. I was an adult. No way in hell could I say, 'Oh, I'm so sorry I can't take this huge step in my career because my brother forbids it.' I couldn't say everyone admired my talents just as long as I anonymously submitted for galleries and didn't put my name on any of it. I couldn't very well say that my brothers supported my 'hobby' as Roman called it but balked at me having a real job that didn't involve twiddling my thumbs.

No. I couldn't say any of that, so I'd said none of those things. Only that she should keep me in mind if she had anything near Paris in the next week. And low and behold, she'd emailed me back that some kids in the city of éité, right outside of Paris were using art as environmental protest.

It was a risk, yes. But lucky for me, I had a whole new team of bodyguards. After all, I'd done that dozens of times, gone on assignment with hulking goons surrounding me. It wouldn't be any different now.

Except someone shot at you.

Despite the steamy heat, a shiver ran up my spine. There could be danger, but that's what Kannon and his team were there for. I didn't want to add to the risk of their jobs, but I'd listen to all protocols, and we were heading out anyway.

And I really, *really* needed to feel like me, even if only for five minutes with my camera. Not the me my aunt told me to be. Not the me my brothers demanded I be, but the *real* me.

All I wanted was to be free, to find a purpose that wasn't wearing a crown and cutting ribbons. *You've found it.*

Except to Roman and Aunt Rebecca, it wasn't *suitable*. But I knew there had to be some kind of middle ground. I'd seen other royals achieve it. I just had to figure out my way.

I'd put my life into my charities and to helping others, but at the same time, it wasn't enough. Nobody saw past the tiara.

And now I was in the position of securing a royal line for my country. What complete and utter bullshit. What I wanted to know was why no one was rushing to pull out the mail order brides for Breck or Wilder. Women fell over them constantly. Surely one of them could have impregnated someone. Hell, knowing Breck, he probably already had.

I turned off the water and slicked my hair back.

Kannon had mentioned that we might be heading out after I took a shower, and I was trying to focus. I couldn't quite believe that this was what was happening in my life. I'd dealt with threats before. I'd had to deal with security since the time I could crawl. No, long before that, when I was an infant, safely tucked into my mother's arms with security on either side of her.

I'd always had someone trying to protect me, someone saying they knew what was best to keep me safe.

And yet, it was different now.

Maybe it was because of the bullets that had been flying at me.

Or maybe it was because of *who* was trying to protect me.

No, I was not going to think about that.

Just because Kannon happened to look like some kind of hot Viking with his build, bright blue eyes and tousled blond hair, that didn't mean I needed to act as if he was the only attractive man I had ever seen in my life.

Lies. He's the most beautiful man you've ever seen.

Over six feet tall with shoulders I couldn't see around. The kind of Superman-like square jaw that made even the handsomest of aristocrats jealous. He was beautiful. And I was sure the idiot knew it. He had that kind of casual confidence that came from being gorgeous and athletic his whole life.

I didn't have time to think about the way he felt against me when he kept me steady. Or the way the corner of his lips twitched when we bantered. Not like I had time for that.

I had more important things to consider.

Like getting home safely. Keeping my brothers safe. And not having to become a baby-maker for king and country.

I knew from the bottom of my heart that my brother would never let that happen, but he might renounce the throne if he had to.

And that was something *I* would never let happen.

Roman might be stoic and sometimes grouchy. He might shout and at the same time act cool and distant.

Yet I knew he had a soft heart. Buried deep, deep down where others might ignore it.

And I knew why he buried it, but that wasn't something we talked about.

All three of my brothers would protect me until the end of their days, but now it was my turn to protect them. By not going back until that stupid rule was taken care of.

But if I needed to, I would go back, and I would protect *them*.

But first, I needed to protect myself.

I *could* protect myself.

And damn Kannon anyway.

I sighed and looked down at my things. There wasn't much to choose from. I'd been more concerned with my lenses. I'd only put a change of undergarments, leggings, and two T-shirts in my bag. The rest of the room was taken up by camera equipment, passports, and cash.

I glowered at the clothes on the bathroom floor. I had passed out the night before and still wore what I had been wearing the day I traveled to Paris. It wasn't a good look.

My wet hair clung to my brow, and it had tangles in it.

Inside the bundle of clothes was my toiletry kit, and for that I was grateful. I at least had my leave-in detangler so I could work on the bird's nest that was my hair.

The scent of home filled me as soon as I sprayed my ends, and I relaxed marginally.

I could do this. I was stronger than this. I wouldn't panic. I would get home and tell the council they could shove their rules.

I had been a good girl and had done what I was told for far too long.

I was not going to breed for the sake of the monarchy.

Aunt Rebecca would help. I knew she had meant

well with her suggestion about the duke, but that didn't mean I had to like it.

She had been the only one I could really rely on for most of my life. When my parents died, I didn't really have anyone else to confide in. My brothers had been just as broken as I was and had gone off in different directions to heal. At least that's what I had figured. It wasn't like we actually talked about it.

Because talking about your feelings was not what a Waterford did.

Aunt Rebecca had been stern, set in the old ways, but had always listened. She had helped to raise me. And she would stand by my brothers and help me get out of this situation.

I just hated that I wasn't there to deal with it myself. Well, that was going to change. As soon as I could, I would deal with it.

As I detangled, the echoing sound of the bullets pinging against the car ran through my mind again, and I shivered. This time, it had nothing to do with pleasure.

I could have died. If whoever had shot at the car had actually been after me, I could have died.

And I had Kannon to thank for saving my life.

ONCE MY HAIR WAS DETANGLED, AND I'D moisturized, I looked around for my underwear.

I must've dropped them on my way into the bathroom. *Crap.*

I cursed, but I hadn't heard anyone come in, so no one should be out there.

I'd be safe.

I quickly opened the door and spotted my lacy black thong on the floor, sitting there and mocking me.

I tiptoed out there, acting as if I was a thief in the night attempting to steal my own underwear.

As soon as I took three steps though, I collided with a very hard, very warm, very *shirtless* mountain.

"Oh my God," I whispered.

My towel fell to one side, and I gripped it around my front, but the side that fell exposed my ass and my side.

I had one hand on the towel, keeping my breasts covered, and the other went to his chest.

I looked up, way up, at Kannon, who just stared down at me, his eyes molten.

"What. The. Fuck?" he whispered.

I could feel the heat of him, not just through the towel but also from his hand on my ass.

He had apparently reached around to steady me as I ran into him, and now his hand was on my bare ass, my skin still damp from the shower, and all I wanted to do was lean into his touch.

My core tightened, and I pressed my thighs together, wondering what the hell was wrong with me.

"I dropped my panties."

Well, that wasn't exactly what I meant to say.

Kannon's throat worked hard as he swallowed. I could see the war in his eyes. But he seemed to be locked in place by the same force that held me there, unable to move. *The pull.* I'd felt it the moment I met him. The instant I'd wrapped my arms around his waist and let the scent of sandalwood envelop me. A fierce, raw connection kept us orbiting each other, and I wasn't sure if either of us could get free.

Kannon stared down at me, his lips parting and his hand tightening ever so slightly on my backside.

I went wet.

And not from the shower.

"You're only wearing a fucking towel, London. I don't see any panties."

"I think they're by your foot," I whispered. Why the hell did I sound so breathy?

"Well then."

I met his gaze again, my mouth going dry.

My belly tightened, and the hand that held the towel shook.

"Well then," I repeated in a whisper.

And then with a low, feral growl, his mouth was on

mine, his tongue thrusting into my mouth, his lips bruising mine.

My fingers dug into his chest, gripping him tighter, and he tightened his hand on my ass, pulling tightly, spreading me.

I arched into him, kissing him harder, the taste of him scorching my tongue.

He tasted of toothpaste and coffee and whatever the hell it was that was all Kannon.

He bit at my lip, and then his other hand went to my hair, pulling the towel as it slithered down my back, causing the terrycloth I'd been wearing to almost fall completely, exposing one nipple and causing it to rub against him.

Kannon pulled away. "Fuck." He turned, his back heaving as he forced his gaze away from mine. "Put on some fucking clothes."

I blinked. Somewhere in my head there were brain cells that hadn't been singed. And any second now, I was going to find words. "W-w-hat was that?" I asked, the coldness at his lack of touch freezing me.

He dragged in a deep breath and turned around, staring up at the ceiling. "Nothing. Go put on some fucking clothes. And panties more substantial than whatever scrap you had near your foot."

He wouldn't move, a frozen statue of heat and molten flesh.

And I stood there with my towel covering only one breast and not much else.

"I...what?"

"Put on some clothes, London."

On his back was a sharp, jagged scar. How had I not noticed that before? "There's a cut on your back," I blurted, just now noticing. I couldn't think through the haze of his touch, and I needed to breathe.

"I know. I was coming in here to put some antiseptic on it. Now put on some damn clothes, princess."

"Let me help with that antiseptic." I was babbling. I needed to do something, *say* something. What the hell had that kiss been about? More importantly, why had he stopped?

"London," he growled. "I told you what I needed you to do."

I licked my lips. "You're hurt because of me. Let me help you."

"You'll help by putting on some fucking clothes." He dragged in a breath. "Now, London." He didn't say that last part as an order. Instead, he whispered it, and then I was able to move.

The pleading in his words shot through me, and I bent down for my panties and ran into the bathroom, slamming the door behind me.

I dropped the towel completely, tossed my panties

on the rest of my pile of clothes, and went to the sink, gripping the edge of the tile.

That had not just happened.

I had not just kissed him back.

It was a mistake.

Liar.

In the mirror, my reflection showed off my flushed cheeks and my dilated pupils. What the hell I had done?

I thought back to the raw, ugly cut on his back and remembered what he had done for me, and I forgot all about the pulsing ache between my thighs.

He had been hurt because of me.

And I was going to fix this.

I quickly brushed my hair out, threw it into a bun on the top of my head, and pulled on my clothes as quickly as I could.

Hopefully he was still out there. Hopefully I could help. Because I refused to be useless.

I walked back into the bedroom, and he was still standing in the corner, this time a couple bandages in his hand, but his chest wasn't heaving as much as it had been before.

"Let me help."

He turned on his heel and glared at me, and I refused to let my gaze go to his mouth, or to anything lower.

Because I had felt the hard, thick line of his erection against me.

And I knew that it was probably going to fill my dreams until the end of my days.

Damn, Kannon.

"You don't have to help me. I can get Olly or someone on my team to do it."

I shook my head. "No, this is my fault. I'll help." I took a step forward and took the bandages from his hand. "I've got this."

He pinched my chin and forced my gaze to his. "It's not your fault I was shot at."

"You sort of blamed me earlier," I muttered.

"That was me being a dick. I was frustrated and pissed off, and I shouldn't have taken that out on you." And then without another sound, he twisted the chair from the desk backwards to straddle it, giving me his back.

"Antiseptic's on the desk. Come on." He swallowed. "I could use the help. And something tells me your touch will be gentler than Olly's."

Then in silence, I cleaned his back. He didn't make a sound, didn't even tighten a muscle, though I knew it had to burn. It was a small cut, something I didn't think would need stitches, but it still had to be painful. Yet every time I touched him, he didn't even flinch. Didn't even let out a breath. I, on the other hand, was all nerves and shaking hands.

What had happened to him that something like this wouldn't hurt?

And why did I want to know more?

Because you're a masochist.

I pressed the bandage over the cut and sealed it and then cleared my throat. "Okay, you're good to go."

"Thanks," he said, softly. Then he stood, and I staggered back. His body and his presence took up so much space. "New plan. We're heading out in the morning. Get settled for the night."

I looked at him and nodded, at a loss for words and hating myself for it. "Oh. Okay. Um...thank you."

"You don't need to thank me for doing my job, princess."

And with that last shot, he stalked off, leaving me standing there like an idiot.

His job.

Got it.

That's what I was to him. A job. Nothing less and nothing more. And that's exactly what I wanted.

Chapter 8
KANNON

It was only supposed to be a job.

JUST A SIMPLE JOB, THEY SAID. IT'LL BE EASY, THEY
said.

But that simple job of watching a debutante had led
me to the far-from-simple princess. Why in the name of
God had I kissed her? Worse, why had I told her she was
just a job? That wasn't the way I ran Kannon Security
at all.

I scrubbed my hand down my face as I chugged
down my coffee. The faster I ate, the less likely I'd be to
linger over breakfast with her.

The only saving grace was that Sparrow wasn't

around to give me shit. Marcus either. The two of them were the biggest shit talkers on the team. Or more like they never let me get away with shit. Marcus had been on escort duty for Little Miss Debutante who was safely back home in Los Angeles now. I'd assigned him to deal with our case load while I handled this job.

I figured between Olly, Sparrow, and me we could provide accurate coverage until we knew who was trying to hurt her. The two of them were mapping out escape routes and weapons. I had Sparrow kitting out a safe house just in case. It paid to be prepared.

The good news was that London hadn't said another word about our kiss.

More like mistake.

That morning she'd woken up and headed straight for the shower, where she'd taken goddamn forever. Not that I was paying more attention than necessary.

When she came out with a towel wrapped around her head wearing a T-shirt and a pair of pajama bottoms I'd given her, she looked...good enough to eat.

That's not helpful, man.

No, it wasn't helpful. Especially since I kept thinking about how soft her lips felt against mine. Her shocked gasp. The way she'd melted into the kiss and the surge of electricity I'd felt throughout my whole body. Like I'd been zapped.

None of that shit was helpful. I tried to stick to the

important things. "Listen, I had some room service brought up. There's coffee, some juice, and pastries."

She practically moaned as she ran over to the tray. "Oh my God, I could eat a horse." She jammed a strawberry into her mouth and the juice trickled down her chin. I wanted to lick it.

Stop looking at her, or this is going to be a fucking problem.

The issue was the taste of her was still on my tongue. I turned away and finished packing up my things. I preferred to unpack methodically whenever I went somewhere. Putting things away like I would at home helped me settle quickly. It was part of the routine. Maybe I was just anal.

London, it seemed, was far less methodical.

She'd tossed her T-shirt over a chair. Dropped her shoes where they were. For a woman who had barely anything on her when I found her, she'd found a way to somehow *expand*.

"Listen, it's probably not safe to stay here much longer. There are CCTVs all over the city, and very likely, a camera caught the two of us walking in here night before last. I've arranged for a safe house."

She wiped her chin with the back of her hand and spoke around a mouthful of chocolate croissant. "No, that won't be necessary. I told you, my friend Rian is expecting me to stay at her house in the country."

She had to be kidding. "With all due respect, your friend won't have the kind of security that I can provide."

"From the look on your face, it seems that you're insistent on staying with me. You'll see that she's got a security system and alarms. There's no reason I can't stay at her place."

I glowered at her. "I haven't scoped out the place yet, so right now I say it's not safe."

"I'm not a prisoner, am I? Roman hired you to keep me safe, not to keep me prisoner."

I frowned at that. "It's for your own safety."

"You can't just force me to do what you want because my brother hired you. I said I'd follow your orders, but I still want to know where you plan to take me. I can get a cab outside the hotel right now and head over to Rian's without you." She paused. "And I have a stop to make before I get there."

My brows lifted as a chuckle tore out of my chest. "A stop? You're joking. No."

"I know there is a safety concern. If anyone thought to check, you'd realize I'm no idiot. I know how to be careful. But I promise you I will not play princess in distress."

I studied her. "What's the stop?"

Her eyes went wide. "You're not going to try to stop me?"

I sighed. "Tell me what it is?"

"Oh, uh, my editor, she wanted me to take photos of some youth environmental activists and the art they're making. I can be fast and take most of them from the car. I won't be in the open for too long. And it's on the way."

Her voice was pleading and her eyes soft. An invisible hand squeezed my heart, and I knew I would regret saying yes. But she did have a point. She could get in a cab right now. But that wouldn't be safe. In fact, that would be the last thing I would want her to do.

If you think you can walk away, please share what you're smoking.

She was a major pain in the ass, and I was pretty certain I didn't like her at all. But she had a point. I didn't work for her. I'd do the right thing, make sure she was safe, then get her home as quickly as was safe...and out of my hair.

Sure, you will. That's why you're still thinking about the way she tastes.

I rolled my eyes skyward. How could one small woman be such a royal pain in the ass? "Okay fine. Write down the address here." I shoved one of the hotel's stationery pads in her direction, along with a pen that said *La Mer*. Worse came to worst, I'd call in the big guns and make her brother talk some sense into her if I had to.

Quickly, she jotted down the address.

"While we're at it, memorize my phone number." I wrote it down for her.

Her brows lifted as she chewed around the chocolate croissant. "Why do I need to memorize your number?"

I sighed. "In case we get separated. You will need to find a phone and call me."

"But if we get separated, wouldn't that be because I left you in the dust?" I set my face to glower. Eventually she rolled her eyes but backed down. "Fine, yes, I'll remember it."

I watched as she used her fingers, tapping out the number sequence, and then I lifted both brows. "What are you doing?"

She lifted the notepad. "I'm memorizing the number."

"Yes, I know. But what's with the tapping?"

"My brother Wilder taught me how when I was little. Some kind of number sequencing or something. It helps me make sure that I never forget something."

THIRTY MINUTES LATER, ONCE WE HAD ALL OUR stuff in the car, we headed out toward Rian's house. It was far outside of Paris, definitely more scenic, away from the hustle and bustle of the city. We had driven about forty-five minutes when London started to shift in her seat. "Can we stop at a gas station?" A pause. "I need to use the facilities."

I checked the GPS. We had at least another forty-five minutes before we arrived in Lité. I didn't like it, but if we were smart, I could keep her in the car and keep her safe. "What are the chances that you can wait?"

She sent me a glare.

"Fine. There's a gas station coming up if the GPS is accurate."

When we pulled in, she bolted out of the car in a flash and I started to fill up, keeping my eye on both the road and the small convenience store. There were no other cars around and no easy access behind the place for someone to ambush her. When she came out, the sun hit her hair in such a way that I could see some dark reddish highlights. And then she gave me a beaming smile that struck me dumb and mute for a moment. *Fucking hell.* Her smile was a lethal weapon. "Thank you."

I glanced at the store. "Want something to eat?"

She nodded. "Maybe some water and chocolate bars?"

She turned to walk in herself and I stopped her. "No, I'll go," I muttered even as I rolled my eyes, thinking this was a response Sparrow might give. "Women and their damn chocolate."

"I don't know what to tell you." She reached for her bag, but I waved her off.

"No. I'll take care of it."

She slid into the car, moaning slightly at the soft seats, and I slammed the door shut. Once inside, I made it a point to be quick. No dillydallying. The sooner I could get her to Rian's house, the better I would feel.

While inside, I kept an eye on the mirrors pointed at the parking area, and when I saw something suspicious, I put my plan into action. With quiet steps, I eased open the door without the bell attached. I made sure my footsteps were light across the pavement. Years of training ensured that, but it never hurt to be careful. The element of surprise was key here.

The rush of adrenaline amped up my heart rate and quickened the pace of my breathing, all of which told me I was on the hunt. And I was about to have some fun.

My hand was in and out of my jacket holster in seconds. Then I pressed the barrel against the spine of the man presently trying to yank open London's door and muttered, "It's not nice to sneak up on a lady."

He tried to whip around, but I was faster, waiting for him with a fist. I popped him twice—straight jabs to the nose. He gurgled, exposing his throat. Then I punched him there, leaving him to wheeze and cough as he crumpled. London unlocked the door for me, and I wasted zero time climbing into the driver's seat. "You okay?"

"Oh my God, as soon as you went inside, he came to the door and tried to get me to roll down the window. I wasn't about to, but there wasn't much I could do if he'd decided to shoot it. Damn it."

"You're safe?"

"God, I don't know what would have happened if you hadn't come. He was threatening to shoot at the window. And he kept tapping his gun on the glass. I know it's bulletproof, but I wasn't sure if that counted at such close range."

I calmly but quickly maneuvered the car out of the parking lot and hit the gas. "You're okay. You're fine. Take a deep breath." Her eyes were wide and her breathing far shallower than I would have liked.

"How are you so calm? Did you kill him?"

I frowned. "No. I wish I had, but I didn't."

"What is going on? Why do you sound like you know something I don't?"

"You're the only one who can answer that question."

"I don't *know* why anyone would want to kill me. I'm hardly important enough for anyone to want me dead." She still couldn't grasp it. I could see her panic rising.

"I don't believe that. But look, you're safe now. And

always remember, if you're ever in the car again and someone attacks you, there's a gun in the glove box."

Her brows furrowed. "Why didn't I think of that?"

"Probably because it hasn't been ingrained in your head. But this only leads me to the conclusion that you are absolutely being followed. We're going to get another car, and you're going to dump everything, all of your belongings."

"What?"

"Dump everything."

"But my camera."

The fear in her voice was palpable. "I had Sparrow check it this morning. It's clean. The camera and lenses are clear. Let's kill everything else to be safe."

"But I don't have anything else on me."

I laughed at that. "You're still wearing earrings, a necklace, a watch, and probably a few things I might have missed. If that's what you left home in, a tracking device could have been sewn into the collar of your jacket or planted in anything you have on. And you've got a lot on. And I'm sorry, but Lité is out."

I thought she was going to argue. I thought she'd fight me. But all she did was nod quickly. Her eyes though... The normally vibrant baby blues were clouded with unshed tears.

Christ, she'd been run off a road, people had shot at her, and some idiot had just tried to drag her out of a car. She was holding up remarkably well, considering.

I found the one shopping center I'd seen on the map. I picked a spot in the far corner, just out of range of the cameras. I hated the idea of leaving my car here, but we didn't really have any other options. I scanned the lot's numerous other inhabitants and spotted a vehicle that was just the ticket. A red Peugeot, an older model before all the updates to computer systems, and I knew it would be easy to steal.

I grabbed our gear as soon as I parked. "Start stripping."

"I'm sorry, what? No. I will not be stripping in front of you, especially when I don't have anything to change into. You might have saved my body, but you don't get to see it."

My gaze slipped over her slender frame and paused just long enough at her breasts. It made me want to kick myself. "I'll give you a shirt. Make it fast. We're leaving all of that here."

I transferred my gear between cars quickly. Lucky for me, the Peugeot was easy to hotwire. *Perfection.* Hopefully, her friend had a car available. One that no one had seen us in before.

London had done as she was told. She'd stripped. Down to her bra and panties.

"I said all of it."

She blinked. "The hell I will."

I sighed, grabbed one of my shirts out of my duffel, and handed it to her. It would certainly be long enough to cover her to nearly her knees. "I was serious too. Bra as well. It's easy to hide something in the underwire."

"Will you at least leave me the dignity of my panties?"

I did my best, trying not to think of her panties. It didn't work. Now all I could imagine were her curves in microscopic lace, and my dick ached. "Fine. Make it fast. We've got to go."

She *was* fast. When she buttoned up the last couple of buttons of my shirt, I couldn't help but stare at her. She was like a walking, talking model come to life with her silky hair cascading over her shoulders, her bright blue eyes, and those thick, dark lashes looking up at me. All I could think about was how she tasted and how I was not going to think about that anymore.

Sure.

Once we made the car switch, I made a mental note to tell Olly to come and retrieve my BMW. If I was lucky, he'd be able to find someone to fix the scrape I got in our crash a couple nights ago. Not to mention the bullet holes.

During the rest of the drive to her friend's, London was solemn, quiet. She didn't say a word.

"Are you okay?"

"Of course. Other than being followed and men with guns running me off the road and trying to kill me at rest stops. However, it's not as if I have a choice. So let me put on a pretty smile and pretend if that suits you."

Fuck. "I promise you this situation will get better."

"Let's not make promises we can't keep, shall we?"

She had a point. She didn't know me. She didn't know that if I promised to keep her safe that was my intention. But I was going to do everything in my power to make sure that's what happened.

Are you going to keep her safe just like Phoebe?

Even from my subconscious, that was dickish. "Just relax. We're almost there."

When we switched cars, I'd switched to GPS on my phone. The thing about GPS devices was that they never told you exactly what to expect about the location you were traveling to, with the exception of Google, maybe. You could get a street view, or a satellite view if you had one. But when we pulled up to London's friend's place, I felt like I was at the Guggenheim Museum.

Ultra-modern, weird, funky architecture. A large metal sculpture sat at the top. It looked like a metal wonton. *What in the world?*

The house itself was all white and chrome and steel. "This is your friend's place? Rian?"

She stared up at the building as if she wanted to

smile but it couldn't quite reach her face. "Yep. Rian Drake."

I frowned. Why was that name familiar?

"She was one of *People* magazine's most beautiful last year. The cover, actually. And she won an Oscar two years ago. A Tony, too. Oh, and a Grammy for her movie, *The Wild Children*."

I paused at the entrance of the driveway. "What? Rian Drake? The actress?"

"Yes, she's an actress."

I blinked at her. "So the last two hours we've been driving, you didn't think to mention that your friend with the ridiculous security is a world-famous actress?"

"Her place is private, secluded. No one knows about it. And it's secure to the hilt."

"Way to bury the lead." London rattled off the security code, and I punched it in and drove us into the long drive. Once the gate receded behind us, it rolled back out, and I noticed the electrical panels at the security gate. "What you're telling me is those things go hot when you say they should?"

She shrugged. "I don't know everything about her security, but she told me I'd be able to stay here and feel safe."

Interesting. Had she known she'd need to feel safe before the bullets had flown? "I hope she has a manual for this place."

Chapter 9
LONDON

The princess and the protector

I HAD NEVER BEEN SO RELIEVED TO REACH A destination in my life. I knew I wasn't being dramatic. Being locked in the car with Kannon for two solid hours only made me relive every second of that kiss. *Pure torture.*

Especially as he hadn't said a word about it. Not one. I kept waiting for him to say something, anything. Instead, he was perfectly comfortable not addressing what had happened.

If he could pretend nothing had happened, well, so could I.

It helped that I had more important things to worry about. Someone had tried to kill me. *Twice.* They tried once and then came back around to make sure that I was dead. At least that's the best I could come up with. I needed to talk to Roman again. Maybe he'd found out something that could explain what the hell was going on.

Aunt Rebecca had said there were people who were looking to take the crown from him, from us, but would they resort to murder? And hello, I was hardly in line to rule. Roman would eventually recover from the loss of Kissa, and he would marry. It would just take time. And then both Breck and Wilder were ahead of me. I was basically a commoner. Why anyone would care what the hell I did or if I had a child was beyond me.

You heard it with your own ears. You have a year to have a baby, or the royal line changes.

I hoped to God my aunt was being dramatic, but she'd had real fear in her eyes. My father's sister had looked out for us since our parents died. She'd always been there. Always guiding.

Roman had been so young. Only twenty-two. When most men his age were sowing their wild oats and making mistakes, he'd been left to run a country. And the rest of us, well the rest of us were just unruly. The boys were the worst, of course. No one wanted me to be like Princess Stephanie of Monaco, so I had been reared with firmer hands. But I was still independent as hell.

If there was real danger, Breck would have been all over it. He would have been the first to warn me. *No, my brothers didn't know when they helped me escape.* As soon as we were settled, I needed to find a phone and call them.

As we pulled up to Rian's house, even my jaw went slack. I was used to her Paris flat. While well-equipped and gorgeous, and spacious for Paris, it was *still* Paris. Comfortable, but not overly roomy. Not like this. This was like something you'd see out of a James Bond film or some Malibu estate.

There was a piece of architectural art on top of the roof. It looked like a giant platinum wonton. I remember her telling me that when she'd built this place, she wanted a serene yoga retreat. Was it up there? I was a sucker for green spaces, but I couldn't see anything outside of the gate really. But that giant wonton, *that* was visible. As was the whole top floor of the home.

When I told Kannon the code Rian had given me, he typed it in, and the massive metal gate swung inwards. Inch by inch, as the gate revealed more of the yard, more of the property, I gasped. Kannon just cursed under his breath and gave a low whistle. "Wow. This is... something else."

"I have to say even I'm surprised. When Rian said she had a place outside of the city too, if I preferred, I didn't realize it would be something like this. I really thought I'd stay with her in Paris."

Nothing was going as I'd thought, but it wasn't as if I had a real plan. Only to run from royal decrees I had no part of until my brother could figure it out. I hated the fact that I couldn't do it myself. But I'd find a way. I could be my own savior.

I refused to look at Kannon.

He's saved me. More than once.

I hated that I couldn't do it myself.

The gates opened to a sprawling massive green that was perfectly maintained and cut. There were patterns cut into the grass. I couldn't tell what they were from our vantage point, but there was clearly a pattern there. The drive was long and wound up to the house. And as we drove, I could see that there were several structures behind the main house.

We parked outside the garage, and then Kannon took a call. When I stepped out of the car, eager to grab a bag, I frowned. I had no bag. I had on Kannon's shirt and a pair of panties. And my shoes. At least, I had my bloody shoes. I hadn't thought to ask if I should ditch them or not. But surely, they were fine. They were just a pair of ballet flats. Completely innocuous.

With nothing to grab or carry, I strolled up to the front entrance, marveling at the bougainvillea and the roses scenting the air. They were gorgeous. Her landscapers were impeccable and amazing. I could see on the side of the house that there were massively large hedges leading farther along the property. Maybe there was a maze garden of some sort?

Kannon's voice behind me was low. Gruff. "My team will be here in thirty minutes."

I jumped. "How do you not make a single sound when you walk behind me?"

"I'm not *that* quiet. You were just lost in thought. You need to be more aware of your surroundings. Situational awareness is important."

I rolled my eyes, though I knew he was right. Damn him. "Of course. Make sure you take every opportunity to put me down."

He frowned. "I'm not putting you down. I'm just making a point. You know the situation is already stressful."

The house was all steel and chrome and white. The front wall was mostly windows. Floor to ceiling. The place had amazing natural light. I punched in the key code I'd been given for the front door, and something clicked. Then I pushed the heavy door in.

Despite the chrome and steel, Rian was still Rian.

The floors were gorgeous. The rich acacia wood instantly warmed the space. The foyer was brightly lit with a massive chandelier hanging above. Crystal probably. Swarovski? To the right was a massive sunken living room. The walls were an eggshell color, and Rian had paintings and photographs on every inch of them. The furniture was a massive white sectional, but there were a couple of fun throws on it that looked like an African print as well as brightly colored pillows that matched the colors from the throws. Just being in the space, I missed her. Everything about the place screamed, 'Hey, Rian designed me painstakingly.'

On the left, there was a library, and I couldn't help but grin. I remembered in college that Rian always squirrelled books away. She insisted she needed them. Even several copies of some books because she said you never knew when you were going to need a story to carry you away. I was disappointed that she wasn't here. When I'd used Kannon's phone to send her a message that I was in Paris and delayed even more than her, I told her I wasn't going to make it to her flat and was wondering if I could stay in her house in the country. She'd said, 'Absolutely.'

"London? I'm going to leave you alone here for a moment and check on the security. Okay?"

I searched his gaze for a moment. He looked like

maybe he wanted to say something, but he didn't. He was so close I could feel his heat. The fire and energy that crackled between us was dangerously overwhelming, but he stepped away.

I nodded, not sure what to say.

"I'll be right back."

I was left with nothing to do but explore. Walking down the hallway, I finally found the kitchen and dining room. It was a massive open space. And from the dining room, there was an archway into another living space. The kitchen was something a chef would dream about. It had all kinds of pots and pans I didn't know the names for. There was also a massive island with what looked like a marble countertop, but Rian was practical. She liked red wine too much to have marble because it was porous and stained too easily. I figured it was probably granite or something, but it was gorgeous, no matter the material.

In the kitchen, nestled on its charging dock, I saw an iPad. From staying with Rian before, I knew she kept devices around everywhere, making sure everyone had access to the internet. I logged in with the familiar passcode from her Paris flat, and sure enough, it worked. Immediately, I called her on FaceTime. It rang several times, but then she finally answered. "London, is that you?"

Oh, my God, I hadn't even realized how much I

needed to see her face. The relief flooded my veins. There she was, *Rian*. Something about Rian's broad smile always made me feel better. Her smile always lit up the entire space. When I saw her on Broadway the previous year, her presence had commanded the whole theater just by walking out on the stage and beaming that smile. "Hey, gorgeous. Yep. It's me. In the flesh."

"Oh good. I'm glad you're settled in the house. The guest rooms are open and available thanks to the caretakers. You can use the guest houses too, if you want. A little privacy from each other, of course. You said you're travelling with a friend?"

I cleared my throat. "Um, something like that."

She lifted a perfectly arched brow. Her warm cocoa skin was perfection, as usual. High cheekbones, completely without any blush or makeup, yet she looked flawless. I looked like a bedraggled swallow that had fallen out of her nest. "It's a long story, but I needed to get out of Alden for a minute. You know how the brothers are so overbearing. For my birthday, I decided to come visit."

"Oh, love. I'm sorry I'm not there. Filming ran long on this shoot. But I'll be back in a week. When I'm back we will drink wine, talk men, and discuss projects. I remember you saying there was a company you were waiting on to see if they'd hire you to do a photo series on the Amazon bush fires, right?"

This was why I loved Rian. Despite having all the world often focused on her, despite being surrounded by a gaggle of men, she always remembered and made sure to ask about the real things that mattered. "I'm waiting to hear from them. I mean, it's kind of a long shot. I don't have that much experience or a huge portfolio, but I'm hoping."

"Obviously, I'm sure your family could make some calls, but we don't want that. Better you do it on your own. That way, no one can come and take it from you."

"Exactly. I love that you understand."

"I've met your brothers, and I know you."

Behind me, I heard a voice that was all steel. "Just who the hell are you talking to?"

"Oh my God, Kannon, this is Rian."

I turned the device over so he could see her face. It was funny watching him do a double take and blink. "Um, uh, ma'am?"

Rian wrinkled her nose. "Oh my God, you did not just call me ma'am. Call me Rian."

"All right, Rian, it's nice to meet you."

Rian grinned at him, and her eyes were wide and glittering. "Nice to meet you too..."

"Kannon. I'm Kannon."

"Excellent, Kannon. Just how did you and London meet?"

Kannon's gaze lifted to mine and narrowed. "This is

my cue to duck out." He moved remarkably fast for someone so big.

Rian lifted a brow. "Looks like you're left to tell the tale."

"It's an unusual story, but suffice it to say that only in Paris would I meet a man who can help me when I need to find somewhere safe."

Rian's eyes narrowed. "Safe?"

"I'm fine," I lied. I didn't want to worry her more than she probably already was. "But he's just a...friend."

"A hot friend," she teased, but I knew Rian was still worried.

I held back a smile even as I tried to hide anything she could latch on to and worry about. "It's not like that."

Rian's brow furrowed. "It's not like what? You met somebody fine. You needed a place to stay away from the city. It's so romantic."

"To be fair, I never said I needed it to be romantic."

"I'm just teasing you. Well, whoever your new, uh, friend is, he's very cute. And I encourage you to jump into the world of dating."

"Rian, you know he can hear you."

She grinned. "You're the one who put me on speaker."

I rolled my eyes. "Thank you for letting me stay here. Um, do you have all the security manuals and stuff for this place? I want to make sure it's all locked up securely if we need to go out."

From where he was standing, Kannon gave me a thumbs up. At least he was happy with the way I was handling that.

"There's a full manual in the library desk, bottom drawer. There's also a secondary manual in my bedroom bedside table, bottom drawer. Do not look in the top drawer."

I coughed a laugh. "Yes, ma'am. Thank you again for everything. I need to go now, though. I want to shower. And I'm sure you're very busy."

She rolled her eyes. "Last week of filming. Everything is tight and tense here. But mostly it's hurry up and wait. I've been in my trailer for hours, so thank you for breaking up the boredom. I miss you, and I hope I get to see you in a week."

I hoped someone stopped shooting at me before week's end.

"Me too. Love you. Talk to you soon."

"Oh, and London?"

I lifted a brow. "Yes?"

"Have fun. I know it's been in scarce supply lately."

I laughed. "I hear you."

When I hung up with her, Kannon came back in. "The place has got really good security. I'll take a look at the manuals. I think my team can figure it out, but it will be helpful to have all the instructions."

"Great, thanks." I didn't know what else to say. I was so far out of my depth right then, I felt useless, something I never wanted to feel again.

When he went to go and find the manuals, I made one more call. It was Roman who answered, a scowl on his face.

"It's about time. Are you safe?"

I didn't know why that scowl made me so happy. I missed him. "I'm safe at Rian's. Kannon and his team are on the job."

My brother studied my face. "What else happened that you're not telling me?"

"I'm fine, Roman. We're figuring out what to do next."

"I'm sending an update in a few minutes," Kannon said from behind me, making me stiffen.

"Good," Roman spoke over me.

"I'm right here," I said, trying to remain calm while they talked around me.

"You are. And we're working on keeping you safe." Kannon met my brother's gaze. "You working on what you need to on your end?"

"Yes."

That was all my brother said before he turned his

attention back to me. Cryptic was a family trait when it came to my brothers, apparently.

"Stay safe, London," Roman whispered.

"I'm trying. What can I do from here to help you?"

"Nothing," he said, and I deflated. "Just be safe. You'll ignore this but stay out of trouble."

Then he hung up, and I was staring at a black screen, wondering how the hell that had happened.

"You done making calls that could potentially let people know where the hell you are?" Kannon said, his voice tight and full of gravel.

I narrowed my eyes before turning and jabbing his very large chest with my finger. "I told you I'd stay put because I'm not an idiot. But now I'm in a safe place. My brothers will send our people. I'm good. You can go. You've done your duty. Mission accomplished. That's what you care about, right? The mission?"

I was aware of how close he was then. I'd been jabbing him, but he hadn't moved. Instead, I'd only been bringing my body closer to his.

Danger, Will Robinson, danger.

The tension and electricity crackled and swirled around us. His gaze dipped to my lips, and I could feel the hum of desire beneath my skin, making it tight and itchy. Making me want to rub myself all over him.

What is wrong with you, London? Get it together.

But I couldn't. For the last several years, I'd haphazardly dated. No one really catching my interest. No one I really trusted to want me for me. No one I felt any pull to whatsoever. But this man. I wanted to throw things at him while simultaneously wanting him to lick into my mouth again. Why *this* guy? For the most part, I liked men who were refined, cultured, handsome, of course, but I'd never been one to fall in love. I wouldn't exactly call myself a hedonist. Every single one of the men I'd dated had always treated me like I was too ambitious for my situation, which was BS. But Kannon... *Kannon* lit my skin on fire, and I didn't know what to do with that.

"You're too close."

"You are free to move, princess."

"Stop calling me that."

"Well, you are a princess, aren't you? A spoiled, pampered rich girl who doesn't have to follow any rules, right?"

"You don't know me. You think you have any idea who I am? God, you're just a giant pain in the—"

"You talk too damn much." And with that, his lips slammed down on mine.

Molding over mine in a perfect fit. Again, I'd like to pretend I stood shell-shocked for a moment. I would like to pretend that I even put up some kind of fight. I would like to pretend that I hadn't been completely malleable and easy, but that would be BS. Total and utter bullshit. I didn't fight. I didn't put up any kind of resistance at all.

Instead, I closed my eyes and savored the sensation of his lips on mine, having missed the contact.

His tongue delved into my mouth, stroking and licking. Mine danced in partnership with his, desperate for more, greedy, needing him. He backed me up against the counter and then he bent down slightly. His hands were suddenly on the backs of my legs as he hoisted me up onto the counter. Stepping between my knees, he angled the kiss better. My legs wound around his waist, bringing him closer. Oh so close. I could feel the hard length of him pressing against my cleft, and I couldn't help but shudder. *God, yes. This* was what I needed. *This* was what I had been hoping for and needing, and... Oh my God.

He made a low growl in the back of his throat. He slid his hands into my hair, fisting gently, angling my head, completely taking over the kiss. My hips rolled into his, and another of those low groans rumbled against my chest.

Then my hands were on him, sliding up over his chest, over and around his shoulders, stroking every muscle. I slid my hands into his hair, my nails scoring his scalp. I could feel the shudder run through his body, and I almost smiled in satisfaction.

His hands slid up over my hips, under the hem of the shirt I wore. His thumbs gently grazed my belly before bracketing my ribs. Slowly, slowly inching up. I arched my back in silent invitation. God, I needed to just...if he could just—

And we had lift off.

He palmed both of my breasts, kneading them gently. And I could feel the pulsing straight down in my core. I rolled my hips over his erection again, and he met me roll for roll. One of his thumbs stroked my nipple, and I tore my lips from his. "Oh my God."

He captured my lips again quickly as he continued stroking my nipple, pinching it lightly. The pleasure pulsed between my thighs and I could feel it. I was coming. That blissful heat chasing up over my spine, it was coming. I was so goddamn close. One of his hands slid away from my breast and scooped down over my ass, bringing me closer against him, making sure there was no room between us. That I had nowhere to escape.

Yes. This is what I had been craving during that whole drive from the city. This is what I'd hoped would happen last night without even knowing it. This was what I wanted. *Kannon.* With his hands all over me and his mouth on me, and—

"While it's totally hot watching you two grope each other, we have work to do. Bone on your own time."

Kannon whirled around. He had a gun in his hand. *Where had that come from?*

I whipped my head around to find the woman I'd seen back at the hotel. The one Kannon called Sparrow.

Now I was able to see her more clearly, and she was gorgeous. She was shorter than me. More average height. Her hair was dark and glossy, her skin a light brown. She also had the kind of cheekbones that made women jealous. Her eyes were wide-set and seemingly missed nothing. Her hair was pulled up into a high ponytail, and she wore a cheeky grin, displaying even, white teeth.

A shuddering breath tore out of Kannon. "Jesus Christ, Sparrow, I could have shot you."

"Hardly. You didn't even hear Olly and me come in." The woman smiled and waved at me. "Hi, I'm Sparrow. I work for him. We didn't get to chat at the hotel earlier."

Kannon turned back to me. His gaze landed on my lips once more, and then he backed away. His grip was firm on my waist as he picked me up as if I weighed nothing then settled me gently on the floor. "Formally then, London, Sparrow. Sparrow, London. Sparrow's number one on my team."

"How big is the team?"

"Total six. She's one of my best bodyguards."

I eyed her. She was small, but something about the glint in her eye told me that she was more than capable. I gave her a shy smile. "Hi. Sorry about this."

She shrugged. "I'm just shocked to learn that Mr.

Truth and Justice also has a heart. No one is going to believe this."

Kannon scrubbed a hand over his face. "Christ, Sparrow, come on. Cut me some slack. Did you bring what we needed?"

She slid him a glance that fully said, *"You're busted, sucker."* But she turned around and opened a bag she'd placed on the island and then dumped out several things. "Olly is bringing the rest of the clothes inside."

She turned her gaze to me. "I think I got your size right,"—she snickered—"but Kannon will have to tell me if your bra sizing is correct."

Kannon growled. "Sparrow, that's enough."

She giggled. "I'm just saying. Last night, you told me 34C. But now that you've had the chance to further explore, is that accurate?"

My skin heated. "Oh my God, I'm actually a 32D, but it's fine. I'm sure whatever you got will work. I can just wear sweatshirts."

"Also, I've got a wallet in here for you and a new phone. It's a burner, but it'll do for now. And some hair products. I didn't have anything fancy. Just a few things to get you through."

"Thank you. My friend, this is her house, she's taller than me, but we're about the same size, so I have other options too."

Sparrow nodded. "Well, I'll leave you two kids to

sort yourselves out. Or bum, you know. But, boss, you might want to clue us in on security before you get back to your extracurricular activities." Then she turned and sauntered out of the kitchen.

Kannon's gaze snapped to mine. "That can't happen again."

I stared at him. "Oh, don't worry. It won't."

Chapter 10
KANNON

You can run, but the past can't hide.

AFTER EXTRICATING MYSELF FROM LONDON AND getting the security brief from Olly, I tried my level best to stay the fuck away from London.

I was an idiot. But none of that was new. Twice now, I'd put my hands on London. It didn't matter what I told myself... She'd start talking and we'd start arguing. And then I'd forget that kissing her was a terrible idea. Never mind that she was a princess and that I'd met her less than forty-eight hours ago. Oh, and some assholes wanted her dead, so I had more important shit to think about.

I was better than that.

Jesus Christ, the last time I had gotten close to someone I was supposed to protect, it ended in blood and screams.

That wasn't going to happen again.

And it sure as fuck wasn't going to happen to the Princess of Alden.

I paced around the monstrosity of a safe house and shook my head.

My team was on it, doing what they could to keep her safe, as well as coordinating with the royals back in her country.

Nothing seemed out of the ordinary there, other than an arcane rule that was going to make London a breeder.

I held back revulsion at that thought.

It wasn't my business, and while her brothers seemed to be doing their best not to have to bend to that rule, London was on the run because of it.

And people were after her.

I hadn't imagined those gunshots. Hadn't imagined the threat. I needed to make sure London was safe. And then I'd walk away. Because I wasn't going to fucking kiss her again.

"Why are you growling in the corner?" London asked, a frown on her face.

Speak of the devil and she shall appear.

I glowered at her. "I'm not growling."

"You literally just growled the words, 'I'm not growling.'"

I narrowed my eyes. "I don't know what you're trying to say. I'm watching the perimeter and keeping you safe. And if you'd stay away from the fucking windows, that would help me out."

She raised a regal brow and looked pointedly over her shoulder.

"The blinds are shut. Sparrow already came through and gave me the spiel. Why are you acting like a dick?"

"I'm acting like the guy your brothers are paying to keep you safe. If you don't like my attitude, then go to your fucking room and stay away from me."

She narrowed her eyes at me, folding her arms over her chest.

Once again, I did my best not to look at her tits.

Liar.

It wasn't easy.

I remembered the exact shade of her nipples, that gorgeous dusky pink, the way the water had slid down in between her breasts when her towel had fallen.

I could still feel the softness of her skin and the thickness of her ass when I spread her cheeks.

And now I was hard, and I was pissed off. I wanted her. She knew I wanted her. But just my luck, she was only having a bit of fun with me. Slumming it with the bodyguard.

Get it together. You're not a teenager. You have self-control.

My heart rate increased. "You think maybe for the rest of the day we can give it a rest? I'm not in the mood."

She lifted a delicately arched brow. "Excuse me? You're the one acting like a dick. What is wrong with you?" she asked. I heard the hesitation in her tone.

I knew I was hurting her. But if I didn't, she wouldn't go away. And I needed her to fucking go away. Far away from me. She'd get hurt and I couldn't carry that guilt on top of the other guilt.

"You said you'd do what you're told. Now do it."

"I said I would do what I needed to do to stay safe, and I would listen to your rules for that. But you going hot and cold on me? No, we're not going to do that."

"I don't think you have a choice in the matter."

She shook her head and came forward. Thankfully, she didn't touch me. As it was, I could already feel the heat of her, and if she put her hands on me? I wasn't sure what I would do.

"No, we're going to talk this out. The thing between us."

"We don't need to. Nothing is going on between us."

Hurt showed on her face, but I ignored it. I had to. I needed to be the asshole. I needed to push her away.

Because every time I looked at London, I didn't only see *her* face.

And every time I heard her voice, there was another entwined with it.

And I'd be damned if I let what happened before happen again.

"No," she said. You don't get to do this. You're the one who kissed me. More than once. You're the one who had your hand on my ass. You're the one who wanted more. And now what? You get caught by your team, and now I'm not good enough?"

How could she think that? "This has nothing to do with my team."

"Of course, it does. It has to do with everyone but you."

"I don't even know what that means," I muttered.

"What it means is you are running hot and cold, as I said, and I don't know why. I get I'm not the woman you want. Fine. You're not a guy that I would usually date either."

I ignored the barb.

"Maybe you should just go fuck that duke then and begin making the babies. That would make things easier for you."

She blanched, and I knew I deserved any slap that

CARRIE ANN RYAN & NANA MALONE

came my way. Only it didn't. She just stared at me, kind of studying my face.

I hated it.

She saw too much. For a spoiled, pampered princess, she could see beneath the layers. Maybe that was because of the job she wanted. After all, she needed to see people through a lens in order to pull out the truth of her subject matter.

But I wanted no part of that.

I wasn't her subject. She wasn't pointing a camera in my face.

"Sparrow brought you your camera. Go take some pictures and get out of my hair."

"Why are you acting like such an ass? What the hell is wrong with you?"

"Nothing's wrong with me. I'm not that duke, so why don't you just back the fuck off?"

I needed her to go. Because if she didn't, I'd lean down and touch her. I'd need her. And I couldn't.

Because even wanting her was a betrayal. And I knew that. And just looking at London reminded me of that fact.

"No. This isn't how it's going to work around here."

"You may be royalty on your little island, but I'm the one in charge here."

"And you don't get to talk to me like that just because you're the one with the dick. Remember, I wasn't the only one with my tongue down someone's throat. So tell me, why are you trying to push me away? I know you don't want me. Or at least you don't *want* to want me. Fine. I get it. But why are you lashing out like this? Because it's not going to work for me."

I didn't say anything, just tightened my jaw and glared at her.

Fuck. Fuck. Fuck. I wanted this conversation to end. I wanted her away from me.

"Tell me," she pleaded, her eyes wide. "It's just you and me. Sparrow and Olly are in the guesthouse."

And then she put her hand on my chest, and I was lost. I was clearly already failing at ignoring the pull.

I stepped away from her touch. I couldn't think when she touched me. And if she wanted to see all the ugly bits, it would be easier if she wasn't touching me. Tempting me to break the rules I'd put in place to protect everyone. "Fine, princess. You want the story? Life isn't about castles and people protecting you."

"I know that."

"Really? Doesn't feel like you do. Because you know what? Sometimes people aren't protected, and sometimes it's my fault."

"What happened, Kannon?"

"You want to know? You want to know why whatever the hell you think might happen between us isn't ever going to? Because I've already done this, and it went badly. Very badly." I knew I was spiraling out of control. I could hear my voice rising.

She blinked up at me, letting out a shaky breath. "What do you mean?"

I threw my hands into the air. "I've already lost someone who I shouldn't have been with. My fucking wife. Is that what you wanted to hear? I was fucking married, London. And she's dead because of me. My child is dead because of me. So no, I want nothing to fucking do with you. Because if I did? You'd just get killed. Just like she did."

"Kannon."

Her eyes filled with tears, and I shook my head. "Don't fucking cry. You didn't even know her."

"The pain in your voice, I know that. I'm so sorry. I didn't know. I'm sorry."

She took a few steps closer and put her hands on my chest again.

"I'm sorry."

I looked away. I needed to.

"Phoebe was pregnant. Our first baby. When someone wanted to get to me, they made sure she knew why she was going to die." Her screams echoed in my head once more, and I swallowed the bile that rose in my throat. "They made sure she called and told me that she knew the bomb was under her seat in her car. I heard her scream, and then there was nothing. Just an explosion."

"Kannon," she breathed.

"Don't. Maybe if I'd just listened to the threats before, she'd still be alive. But no, she's dead. So now I make sure I don't get close to anybody that I'm protecting. Because if I do? And they die? Then that's on me. Even more so than just a job. Princess, you'd better back the fuck away because you're just going to be another number in a long line of people I've let down."

The words rang hollow as I swallowed hard, trying to catch my breath.

Her gaze went soft. She looked at me before she slowly wrapped her arms around my waist and laid her head on my chest.

"Kannon. I'm so sorry."

I held my arms stiffly at my sides, and then, almost involuntarily, they wrapped around her, pulling her close.

My body shuddered, and I closed my eyes tightly, willing the thoughts away.

But she just held me, this princess with the attitude and someone trying to kill her.

She held *me*.

And I was lost.

I wasn't sure how long she held me.

It had been so long since I let anyone get close. Let anyone see the mask slip and show anyone the pain.

It could have been minutes; it could have been hours for all I knew.

Somehow, we'd ended up on the couch, London wrapping herself around me spider monkey style. When she finally lifted her head, her gaze met mine. "I'm sorry you lost your wife."

"Wasn't your fault."

"I know. But you should probably know it wasn't yours either."

I shook my head. "No, I am—"

Her lips pressed together in what I recognized now as her stubborn expression. "No, Kannon, you need to know, you didn't put the bomb there. You can't take on all the world's problems. I know you want to fix it. Trust me, I understand the compulsion. For a long time after my parents died, I thought maybe if I'd somehow gotten them to stay, they'd still be alive. I was feeling sick, and they were going to stay home, but I told them to go. If I'd just played up being sick more, they'd have stayed at home and not been hit by a drunk driver."

How the hell was that even the same thing? There was no way she could have known or stopped the events that happened. "But, London, that doesn't make any—"

I stopped when her brow lifted. "Well, it's hardly the same thing."

"Isn't it? What happened to your wife was a horrible accident. Some psycho targeted her. You didn't plant the bomb. Psychopaths have a way of getting to you no matter what. But the result could have still been the same, and you would have still found a way to blame yourself. You can't carry that around with you."

I wasn't a fan of her brand of logic right now. "If you say so. I bet you're still holding onto your parents though."

She shrugged. "Well, it's harder to shake off than I'm saying, but you have to try. You have a life to live."

My gaze swept over her beautiful face. "And what about you? Have you lived your life?" I knew she was trying to avoid having some idiot's baby. But was there someone she loved? Had there ever been? "You're clearly smart, you're stunning, and you're a princess. I'm sure there have been offers."

She licked her lips then. "Yes, there have been a few, but I don't know, I always feel separate." She gave me a wide smile. "I'm living my life, but maybe not living my best life. It's like I'm some kind of spectator. I give the excuses of not having enough time to date and all those kinds of things, but honestly, I'm just terrified. I work really hard on having just the right image, doing all the right things. Doing what's expected. And I am just terrified of failing everyone. All the time. I mean even photography. My mom was a photographer, and so every picture I take, every time I go out, I want to make her proud."

"I'm sure they're proud of you."

"I hope so. But I don't know, all the living life things are always a little bit out of reach. Because of honor, or duty, and all that jazz. Because, well, it's sometimes easier not to do anything."

"The woman I know is kind of a spitfire and takes no shit."

"Well, that London is far away from home and terrified. So not entirely at my best here."

"Well, I happen to like her. She thinks on her feet, she's strong-willed. Feisty. I think she could have anything she wanted."

She gazed up at me under lowered lashes. Then I could see her tongue peeking out to lick her bottom lip. "You've kissed me twice now. And then you backed off. Maybe you're not over what happened to your wife. But you keep kissing me."

I let out a shuddering sigh and tried to breathe. "I know. And honestly, I can't fucking stay away. Every time I'm around you, my control slips."

"You're trying hard not to kiss me."

"How am I doing?"

Her laugh was light and filled me with warmth. "You're failing miserably."

"Right. Let's work on that." She did that thing with her tongue again, and heat shot straight down to my dick. I swallowed hard. "London, you and me, that's probably a recipe for disaster."

Her gaze searched mine. "I know. It's just you're the first person I've had a real connection to in so long, I can't even remember."

I swallowed hard. "I don't want to want you because I'm terrified you're going to get hurt."

"You see a grown woman in front of you, right?"

My lips quirked into a smile. "Absolutely grown." My gaze dipped down to her breasts. My mouth went dry.

"I'm not sure what the hell is going to happen. Hell, I'm not even sure what I want. I just know how I feel when you touch me. And how I feel when you stop."

How could I tell her that I was scared? That deep down I was afraid that this pull, this connection, was even stronger than the one I'd felt for Phoebe. With Phoebe, there'd been love and experience and trust. I'd known this woman not even a full three days, yet she fired all my instincts to protect her, to take care of her. It felt dangerous.

"Isn't there some kind of law against royalty and commoners?"

"Funny you should ask that. It's one of the laws Roman's trying to change."

I stared at her. "You deserve all the things you want."

"Right now, what I want is you."

I knew what I should say. I knew what I should do. I knew that I should stop and walk away and not touch her again. The problem was, I also knew that I couldn't stay away from her. I'd known the woman for three days, and she already had a claim on a piece of me. I didn't like it. I didn't want it. But it was the truth. And there was no point trying to hide it.

I swiped my thumb over her bottom lip. "Do you know how good you taste?"

"No. But you can tell me."

There it was again, that smile spreading over my face before I could even think about it or control it. This woman, who also drove me absolutely batshit crazy, was quietly working her way under my skin. Claiming a piece of me.

Maybe that was telling me something. You didn't feel crazy over people you didn't care about.

"If you were smart, you'd stay away from me."

"Well, sometimes I do the things that I want, not the things that are expected."

"Last chance, princess. I think you see now that if I

drag you into the bedroom then I'm not going to let you out until well into the morning."

I watched her swallow hard. But her chin lifted, and she met my gaze levelly. "Who says I'm going to let you out of the bedroom?"

With a chuckle, I slid my hand to cup her cheek and then slid it into her hair. This was the first time I was kissing her because I really wanted to, not because my control snapped. This was the first time I was kissing her when she expected it. And instead of a crushing snap of control, I felt the warm easy surge of want and need. Something inside my body reached for hers. And the only thought in my mind was *mine*.

Chapter 11
LONDON

A princess never falls.

I COULDN'T *NOT* TOUCH HIM.

His tongue stoked mine and sent shivers through me. This kiss was different than the others. It was slow and deliberate and not at all rushed. It was all seduction.

At the top of the stairs, he pulled back, his heavy-lidded gaze on me. "Are you sure, London?"

I knew what my answer should be. I knew I should stop this, knew I should pull back. But the truth was I didn't want to. I'd spent so much of my life being some-body's appendage. The sister, the princess, never having an identity of my own. And I knew it was even bullshit to whine about it, because I loved my life. But I was lonely. Ever since Mom and Dad died, I'd felt like I was on an island by myself. I didn't feel the same kind of loneliness that Kannon did, but I recognized him as a kindred spirit. It was like I knew him in the dark, our myriad of pain and disappointment linking us in some way, letting us know that even if there was darkness, we weren't entirely alone.

That link, now, was impossible to ignore. For the first time in a long time, I felt seen. I felt alive.

I wasn't sure about much, but I knew I wanted him. That I wanted this. I nodded. "I'm sure."

"Thank fuck."

His lips slanted over mine once again as he paused in front of one of the doors then kicked it open. He carried me easily to the bed and deposited me in the center. He only eased back long enough to drag his T-shirt over his head before crawling back up my body.

His lips devoured mine as his tongue teased, tasted, and tempted me. It was like he knew just how to coax the right response. Like he was completely attuned to me, made for me, making me feel a hundred percent my real self.

Our kisses were a discovery at first, a slow, tentative awakening. The *hey, how are you doing, nice to meet you, what do you like* kind of thing. If I turn this way, will you respond? If I kiss you here, will you like it? It was the first date of kisses.

There were levels, after all. There was the familiar oxytocin check-in. A given to couples with long-lasting relationships, ones borne out of familiarity and mutual love and respect. But these kisses were always the most thrilling. The first flush of discovery.

But the teasing quickly turned more intense. When he pulled back, his hand fisted my hair again as he dropped his forehead to mine. "What is it about you? I can't stay away."

My voice was shaky when I responded. "No one is asking you to stay away."

When his lips crushed on mine again, gone were the tentative kisses. This kiss, the stroke of his tongue into my mouth, this was all possession, all know-how, all determination to brand and mold and possess.

As he kissed me, he angled my body backwards over the bed, knowing how to make my body hum as if he'd spent a lifetime making me beg.

His big body covered mine easily. From somewhere in the distance, somebody was making a mewling sound. A desperate sound of need, of longing, of begging without using the actual words.

That someone is you. Are you ready to beg?

Electricity sparked through my body, igniting the flame that lit me on fire, leaving only one way to extinguish it, only one answer to the question of what I wanted most in this world.

"Need to feel you," he rasped before burying his face in my neck and breathing deep. That slow, deep inhale made me shudder.

I scratched my nails through his hair, and a wave of lust drowned out any remaining rational thought. When he cupped my breast, he groaned as he palmed me completely.

With every touch, electricity arced between us. I felt like I was being incinerated from the inside out.

Rolling away from me and shifting off the bed, Kannon yanked off his jeans, and my eyes locked on his thick erection. Holy hell. Would that thing fit?

He smirked as he caught me staring, the devil taking full control of his smile. "You like what you see, princess?"

I didn't mean to grin back. I meant to have some self-respect, to play a little coy. But screw that. I *did* like what I saw. And I wanted to touch him. I wanted to taste him.

Kannon climbed back over me and placed open-mouthed kisses along my jawline, the column of my throat, my collarbone. When he dipped to kiss my breasts again, a moan ripped out of my throat just before his lips covered the tip. With his other hand, he teased my free nipple until I whimpered. He continued the path of hot kisses down my stomach, past my belly button.

He wasn't done though. When he settled between my thighs and gave a long, leisurely lick between my folds. I dug my hands into his hair, lifting my hips to meet his questing tongue. But he didn't stop the expert strokes of his tongue except to occasionally nip and suck on my flesh.

I'd never come from someone going down on me. Hell, orgasms were often hit or miss with a partner. It was like the stars had to align perfectly.

But Kannon... He knew every dip to kiss, every curve to touch. His deft thumbs separated my flesh slowly, and he eased a finger into me, murmuring against my flesh. "I can feel it coming, princess. Let me see it. Please, give me that gift."

In that instant, I exploded.

Forget seeing stars, the edges of my vision grayed. Between my thighs, Kannon stilled and squeezed his eyes shut, dragging in deep, even breaths.

I wasn't sure how long it was before I could move again. Before I could lift my head and prop myself on my elbows. Kannon lay on my belly, his enormous hands practically a vice on my hips. "Kannon?" I murmured. I ran my hands through the silken strands of his hair. He drew in a ragged breath at my caress. "Princess, I'm trying to hold onto my control here. Just give me a second."

"Please look at me," I said softly.

He lifted his head and locked gazes with me. There was still some pain in his eyes. And something else...longing?

I urged him up to kiss him and he allowed it. It was so soft, so tender. But when I trailed my fingertips down his body and wrapped my hands around the steel-hard length of him, he tore his lips from mine.

"Oh, fuck, I—" His hips bucked, pushing his straining erection into my hand.

I wiggled out from under him until I was on top then trailed hot, openmouthed kisses along the column of his throat. When I found his nipple, his hips bucked again. With my thumb, I stroked the satin-smooth head of his length, spreading the moisture that had leaked.

Hovering my lips over his erect nipple, I whispered, "Is something wrong, Kannon?"

Something that sounded like a strangled moan tore from his chest, and he dug his hands into the sheets.

"I'll take that as a no." I brushed my lips over his taut nipple and chuckled at the groan that tore from his throat.

He bucked again, digging a hand into my hair, gently tugging my head back. "I swear to God, I—"

I ignored him, instead grazing his nipple and pumping his erection again.

Before I could move, he had me flat on my back again and my hands locked above my head, restrained by one of his.

"Kannon?" I struggled slightly, and he smirked down at me.

"You are trying to make me lose control."

"Is that a bad thing?" I asked as I jutted out my chin in defiance.

Still pinning my hands overhead, he reached over to the nightstand and grabbed a condom. *Why, thank you for being so prepared, Rian.* He tore the foil with his teeth. The look he gave me was a feral one.

"If I release you, will you behave?"

I gave him a sweet nod and batted my lashes. His answering chuckle hit me straight in my lady parts.

Rolling away, he sheathed himself before settling back between my thighs. "What do you know, you can follow directions."

"Only when they're directly related to me having another orgasm."

Chuckling again, he kissed me deeply, and I widened my legs to accommodate him. His erection nudged me, and I moaned as he sank inside.

He dropped his forehead to mine, retreated an inch, then pressed forward again until he was fully seated inside me. My name on his lips sounded reverent. "Fuck, London...."

My gaze met his, and immediately nothing mattered anymore. In that moment, everything was perfect. I felt perfect. I felt safe. I felt like I'd finally found where I belonged.

The corners of his lips tipped into a lopsided smile as he retreated and sank back in. When I clamped my legs around his hips, he muttered curses under his breath.

I nipped his lower lip with my teeth, and he scooped his hands under my ass, lifting my hips to his. The new angle had me sobbing at the pleasure. Only when I murmured his name on a sigh did he stroke into me a final time then cry out my name on his climax.

HOLY HELL.

Kannon Adams had my number. Okay, he'd had it twice if I was going to be an accurate statistician about it.

I'd managed to doze off with his body weight half covering me. Something I never did. And when I woke again, I didn't have any of my usual panic. I just felt warm and safe...and a giant erection at my thigh.

"Kannon..."

"Hmmm, princess? Sorry about him. He just woke up with you right next to me and he's eager to visit again."

My breath lodged in my throat as he slid his tongue over mine. The man showed no signs of slowing down. What kind of crazy stamina was this?

These kisses were different though. He kissed me like he was afraid I'd disappear if he let go. I'd never been the center of a man's attention like that before.

I slipped my hands over his torso, skimming over rippled abdominal muscles and the hard planes of his chest. The sounds he made at my touch were more pain than pleasure, but when I paused, he canted his hips, bringing the hot, hard length of him directly against my heat again.

"Again?" I squeaked.

To hold on and attempt some level of control, I slid my fingers into the thick, soft curls at his nape and gently tugged. With a moan, he smoothed a hand down my back to the curve of my ass and tucked me closer to his body. I rolled my hips into his. "I—you're addictive. I can't stop."

I trembled in his arms. "Then don't."

I shivered as he kissed me softly before shifting me, so my head was closer to the headboard. He then settled his body between my legs, tracing a path of kisses from my lips to my jaw, to the sensitive hollow between my neck and my ear.

Leaning down, he breathed soft kisses on first one, then the other nipple, each responding to his caress by instantly budding into hard little peaks. Focusing his attention on one, he drew the dark bud into his mouth, taking greedy tugs while his thumb teased the other.

I bucked, and my back bowed as pleasure reverberated through my body.

"Yes, I need more. I can't stop." Kannon panted hard. "I feel like I'm on fire. You drive me crazy. You know that?"

Sure fingers slid through my lips, seeking my center, and he met my gaze as he found his quarry. Dark eyes, wild with lust, gazed at me, watching my reaction as his questing finger found the center of my torment.

I cried out as he gently sank into me and he held perfectly still except for his questing finger, gently exploring and retreating, occasionally detouring to swirl around my clit but always returning to delve just a little deeper inside me.

"Jesus, you are so tight. So hot..." He bit his bottom lip as he sank in with two fingers and his thumb traced circles on my clit.

Molten heat spread through my body. I parted my legs to give him even better access to my folds. "Kannon..."

Instead of coaxing a response from me, he demanded one, and my body gave him what he wanted. His thigh wedged between my legs, bringing him in contact with my throbbing clit.

I could feel the heat and hardness of his leg muscles and the friction he applied to my sweet spot. My hips gave an involuntary jerk, and he gave me a satisfied grunt.

He left a trail of buzzing nerve endings in his wake as his hand traveled up my belly, then my ribs, to my breast. His lips slid back over mine as his thumb skimmed the underside of my breast. Another shot of lust hit me hard, and I rocked my hips on his thigh. When he did it again, I threw my head back.

He trailed kisses along my jawline, then dipped his head farther to my neck. He traced a thumb over my nipple, and I cried out. Moisture and heat rushed to my center, and the building need tipped me close to the edge of ecstasy. It wouldn't take much. Just one more stroke from his deft fingers, maybe two.

"Jesus, you are so beautiful," he whispered.

He adjusted his position, so he was between my thighs again. The broad tip of his erection nudged me, and my eyes flew open as my fingers curled into his shoulders. "Condom." My eyes locked on his.

He gave me a wild grin. "Look down."

I glanced down between us, and he was in fact sheathed again. "But when—?"

"I woke up hard as a rock and figured I might be able to make you feel good again."

I tried to bite back my smile. "Presumptuous, but I'll allow it."

He slid just the tip inside me, and my eyes flew open. God he was big. And I was sore. But I knew that would only last for a moment. In seconds I'd be on my way to the holy grail of more orgasms, so who was I to argue?

"Presumptuous, hmm?" He slid in even farther, then stopped, giving me time to adjust. He shuddered and my pussy clamped around him so hard his eyes almost rolled into the back of his head.

"Goddamn, you are so damn tight."

With a whispered curse, he pulled back and then slid forward all the way in one deep thrust. I wasn't capable of coherent thought. All I knew was I wanted more. Needed more. The tingling started in my spine. I could feel bliss reaching for me, and I would promise anything to have it.

My hands slid over his shoulders and down his back to land on his ass. I sank my fingers into his flexing muscles, hoping to speed him up. "It feels so good—don't stop."

And then the chasing was over. The wave of bliss hit

me hard, and I sobbed against his shoulder when I came again. Involuntarily, I clamped around him, shoving him right off the cliff with me.

His final few thrusts were peppered with swears and a tight grip on my hip.

"Fuck! Your pussy was made for me, you know that?" He growled it right in my ear. "It's mine now."

"Kannon."

All I heard as the edges of my vision started to blur again were his whispered words, "All mine."

I woke up an hour later. This time I knew exactly where I was, what I'd been doing, and who I'd been doing it with. I'd made love with Kannon.

Love?

Okay, we'd shagged. That kind of sweet thing that turns dirty quickly. Tripping you into a place that is too scary to look at.

I inched out from under him even as I told myself I wasn't running.

Lies.

I wasn't. I was merely putting some distance between us as I used my brain instead of letting my lady parts do the thinking. I was not now, nor would I ever be, the one-night stand girl.

But didn't you just have one?

Mine.

That word. He'd said it like he meant it.

Do you want him to mean it?

That was the whole point. I didn't know what I wanted. I didn't want him to stay just to protect me. In his arms, I felt like I belonged there. But yesterday he'd told me that the greatest love of his life was lost. He wasn't ready for anything lasting.

And I was fooling myself if I thought he was.

It was better for both of us if I walked away now; otherwise, I was certainly going to get attached.

Too late.

Maybe not. I grabbed my T-shirt off of the floor and dragged it on. If I could get back to Rian's room and grab a shower, I could think more clearly and get some clarity. Falling for my protector was not only cliché, but it could only lead to heartbreak.

And nobody wanted that.

Chapter 12
KANNON

One problem at a time

I WOKE UP...*ALONE.*

Like a fool, my brain automatically reached for London, because like the idiot I was, I truly believed she would be there. But she wasn't.

Did you expect anything else?

I sat up and scrubbed my hand over my face. The princess had gotten cold feet.

Apparently, no one had given my dick the memo. I was rock-hard, still able to smell her all over me. Her faint hint of Chanel Chance lingered, and I could still feel her satiny skin all over my body.

Part of me wanted to go and check on her.

Because you're a sap.

But I knew better. I should have been the one to leave after what we'd done. Last night was just one of those things. And I made a mistake of thinking that connection I'd felt was something tangible. Something real.

It had felt...real.

I forced myself into the shower, even though I was hesitant to wash off her scent. I knew it was best for me. Once I was showered and, at the very least, clearheaded, I went downstairs in the maze of a house to find Sparrow in the kitchen cooking. She was dressed in her usual attire. Black leather leggings and some kind of graphic tee that I was quite certain was flipping me the middle finger. The T-shirt was expertly cut though. It fit her frame. Sparrow liked to give the image of being no muss, no fuss, but I recognized designer details when I saw them.

"Morning, boss. Did you sleep well?"

I gave her a non-committal, "Hm."

Her knowing smirk said she knew exactly what I'd been up to last night. I was surprised she had nothing to say about it though. It wasn't like her to hold her tongue. "Everything checked out for security?"

She nodded. "It was all clear last night. Only a few cars on the main road, but they all went to other properties on the street. Olly added a few extra touches, additional 'eyes in the sky' so to speak. Just in case anyone happens to stick their noses over here, he's got an extra layer of protection. Where's the princess?"

I watched her warily, unsure if there had been a hint of sarcasm when she said "princess," but there was nothing in her expression to indicate it. "I think she's still—"

"The princess is right here."

Every cell in my body froze. I turned slowly to look at London. "Good morning."

Her smile was sunny but distant somehow.

This is what we were doing? Fair enough. Not like last night meant a damn thing to me either.

Liar.

She was the first woman since Phoebe where sex hadn't just been about a workout or getting some kinks out. She was the first connection I thought had gone beyond something physical. But it just went to show that emotions could be deceiving. "There's coffee, you want some?"

Her gaze met mine and then skittered away. "Yes, that would be great. Thank you. Black with lots of sugar."

"I think we can manage that." I poured myself a cup, trying not to think about how she liked her coffee exactly like mine. I didn't understand how people could inhale coffee like it was nectar. It tasted like ass. The only way to drink coffee was to mask the taste. I'd expected her to be some fancy froufrou French press kind of girl or an espresso drinker. *But no, she drinks it just like you do.*

I handed her a steaming mug, and she took it with a soft smile on her lips. When our fingers grazed, she quickly jerked her hand back, nearly spilling the coffee all over herself. "Um... thanks."

I lifted a brow. Last night she'd been all over me, but in the morning light, this was her game? Fair enough, two could play at this. "London, now that you're up, we need to figure out a few things."

She eased herself onto one of the stools at the counter.

Is she okay?

I watched her carefully as she winced, adjusting herself on the seat. Was she sore?

None of your business, since she's pretty much acting like nothing happened.

"Start from the beginning. I know we've already been through this before, but I want Sparrow to hear it firsthand."

At that moment, Olly walked in. He nodded at the sight of me. "Boss."

He gave Sparrow a wink as he stole one of the pieces of bacon off the plate she'd been stacking it on. She whacked his hand. And despite Olly being fast, Sparrow was faster. He winced at the contact. "Aww, I'm a growing boy."

She eyed him up and down. "Stop whining. I'm pretty sure you're done growing."

He grinned then. "Well, I'm a big boy. I need to feed the beast."

She rolled her eyes, and in turn Olly grinned at London. "Good morning. How are you feeling?"

The smile he gave her was professional, but there was something a little too charming about it as far as I was concerned. I glowered at him, and he eased that fancy mouth into professional territory.

"Ah, good thanks. You're Olly, right?"

He nodded. "Sorry, I've been busy setting up security. I didn't get to introduce myself yesterday."

"London. Nice to meet you."

I purposely didn't allow them to start small talk. "London, start telling your story from the beginning, please."

She gave me a look I couldn't figure out before speaking. "As you know, I'm Princess London Waterford of Alden. I turned twenty-nine a few days ago. That's when my aunt let me know about a law that has been in place for, I guess, centuries, that says if there is no royal heir to our line by the time the youngest of the generation turns thirty, the monarchy will be transferred to the next eligible royal family."

Sparrow stared at her from her place at the stove. "But that's like some ancient misogynist bullshit. They can't enforce that, can they?"

London shrugged, though she didn't look too casual about it. She was worried, and hell, so was I for that matter. "That's what my aunt says. On the night I left, she was running through options with my brothers. One was to hurry up and get me married off. An arranged marriage situation, which I was not down for. The other was to call in the Council of Lords to take a vote and have the law revoked."

Olly frowned. "Your brother is the king. Can't he just change the law?"

London shook her head. "No. It's not that easy. He needs the Council of Lords to vote with him. The people elect the council to represent them, so no monarch can get too drunk on his power."

I scrubbed my hand over my stubble. "Okay, what happened next?"

"My aunt tried to get the council to have an emergency meeting, and my brother didn't like the options placed in front of us. And I trust him on that matter. We need to do what's right for our people, not only our family. My brothers got me out of the castle so that no ambitious duke or lord who sits on the council would try and get themselves married off to me. Remove the temptation so to speak."

I frowned. "So running was your brother's idea?"

"I didn't want to marry someone that my aunt picked for me and be forced into royal duties."

"Aren't you a princess? They can't force you," Olly said.

She crossed her arms. "They can. And actually, I'm a photojournalist. I have the occasional royal duties, charity events, ribbon-cuttings, and such things, but Roman is the one with the lion's share of responsibilities. I help him in place of a queen when I'm needed, but my title is the only important thing about me where the court is concerned. I was excited to take a job in Brazil, documenting the environmental work some activists are doing. Then this happened. I got assigned another job in Lité on the way here and then we were ambushed. I checked with my boss and I've been benched until I can become more available. It was my dream job. But then this happened, so everything's on hold."

Was she telling the truth? Was it as simple as that?

I leaned forward. "Okay, so you left home. Your brothers put you on a plane?"

"Yes. Just in case the council tries to call me back and demand that I marry someone. I left with little more than what I could easily carry. We decided not to go with any of the usual safe houses because they're all on record. But luckily, I had Rian for backup."

I wanted to believe her, I did. But something about her story just wasn't quite jiving. Not that I thought she was lying, but the sequence of events seemed off. "What did you do next?"

She studied my face, as if looking for something I wasn't saying, but I kept my expression neutral. "I got on a plane and landed in Paris. And when I was driving out to Rian's flat, everything changed. You found me at that point, Kannon. You know the rest from there."

"So you land in Paris, a place where only three people knew you were going, and someone attacked you?"

She pinned her glare on Olly. "My brothers would never hurt me."

"I'm sure they wouldn't, princess. But what happens if you're dead?"

I didn't like the way Olly said princess. That was what *I* called her.

Jesus. I didn't need to be territorial over the title. She *was* a fucking princess.

"If I die, my brother loses the throne unless one of

them magically produces an heir in the next twelve months. Even if they wanted me dead for some reason, Roman would lose everything."

Olly winced and then lifted his gaze to mine. "Far-fetched and crazy, but I don't think her brothers sent someone to kill her."

I agreed, but I didn't say that. "We don't know anything for sure right now. Was there anyone watching you at the airport? Anyone who would have a vested interest in seeing you dead? Were you followed from, I assume, your palace to the airport?"

She frowned and spread her hands. "I don't know. Wilder was keeping an eye out. He was watching surveillance feeds."

"Why would he be doing that?"

"Oh, he's our Director of Intelligence."

I whistled low. "Okay then."

"My brothers would tell me if someone was watching. They have nothing to gain from me being hurt. It just doesn't make any sense."

She might be right, but I had to explore every angle. "Your aunt, the one who's trying to get the law changed, what's her stake in all of this?"

"None. Everything would go to Barkley."

"Who the hell is Barkley?" I asked.

"My cousin." She winced. "He's a womanizer and sloth, but not power crazy."

Royal Line

Olly glanced at London. "Will your brother give me access to his surveillance?"

"We can see. I can call him."

I shook my head. "No more calling anybody. Olly, see if you can access it the hard way."

Olly grinned. "You mean the easy way? I just wanted to be respectful and ask permission first."

I shook my head. Olly was a whiz with computers. He was that guy who people didn't want to leave their laptop open around. He'd poke around, access your bank accounts, and generally just dick around. Luckily, he was on the side of good, *not evil*. So that was helpful.

I glanced at London. "Now comes the hard questions. Is there a husband or boyfriend that we need to worry about?"

Her eyes went wide. "A husband? No. Didn't I just tell you—?"

I shook my head, cutting her off. "Maybe you *had* a boyfriend. Someone who's not so happy about the new arrangement. Maybe you're seeing someone you're not supposed to be seeing? A commoner or something?"

Her eyes narrowed to slits. "Really? This is what we're doing?"

I shrugged. "I'm sorry. We have to ask these questions." I wasn't sorry at all. I was pissed the fuck off. She'd walked out on me without a damn explanation.

Her lifted brow told me that I didn't have to ask her

181

questions like this. "No. The last boyfriend I had was six months ago. He dumped me because I was too focused on my career. I think he thought that I'd be more of a partygoer. More of a princess's princess. So he found me lacking. Other than him, I've had a few other boyfriends, but those relationships have been over for ages. No one has any scandalous game."

"Thank you for letting us know, but we'll double-check." I glanced between Olly and Sparrow. "All right, we have to figure out who the hell is after her. Leave no stone unturned."

To London, I said, "Things are going to get a little more uncomfortable because we're going to fully deep-dive into your life. If there's something, *anything* you're not telling us, now is the time."

She lifted her chin. "I told you everything I know. I don't know why someone's trying to kill me. I've never done anything to anybody."

I knew that to be a lie. She'd sure as shit done something to me. Somehow, in a matter of two days, she'd managed to wedge herself into a crack in my heart, one that I hadn't even known existed. For my own safety and sanity, I needed to keep her at arm's length.

A few minutes after our meeting, I walked by the sitting room and saw London sitting in there. I almost stopped. I wanted to talk to her. Ask her why she ran.

Had I hurt her? I hadn't let her sleep, that was for damn sure, but she'd been happy when we passed the fuck out.

So why run then? Because she's not for you.

Under my skin or not, I just had to accept that. The princess wasn't for me. So instead of stopping, I shut the door on my heart and kept walking.

Chapter 13
LONDON

A princess never tells.

THANKS TO SPARROW, I COULD AT LEAST WORK. AND avoid talking to Kannon.

He'd clearly been pissed I'd left him in bed.

How would you feel?

I ignored the twinge around my heart. I'd messed up. I'd only needed some time to think. Then I'd been too terrified to go back to bed. And then, well, he'd been pissed.

Just where I was supposed to go from here, I had no idea. In the last three days, my life had fallen to complete shit. And I couldn't breathe. Dealing with the flood of emotions around Kannon was too much to deal with.

You want him. Just say that.

I did want him. But I also had no idea where my life was going. I couldn't examine what I'd started to feel for him.

Sparrow saved me from being in my head too much though. She brought me a laptop, and I was able to log in to my website and clean some things up. I was also able to work on a few emails and replied to the necessary ones. Olly said he'd set up a relay system, so I should be safe enough to not have my IP address recorded. I knew a little about what he was talking about thanks to Breck, so I knew enough to take it seriously. But some of it felt like overkill. At least I hoped it was. If I let myself think it was truly necessary, it would be hard to focus without succumbing to mind-numbing fear.

There was a knock at the door of the library, and I glanced up. Sparrow approached me with a smile.

I took out my earbuds. "Hi. Do you need me for something?"

"I just came to say hello and grab a book. These scenarios are often wait and see with a lot of downtime. And I could use some space to do some research without the boys breathing down my neck."

Sparrow presented an opportunity to glean a little

more information. "Is it just you and Olly who work with Kannon?"

She shook her head. "No, there are four others on the team. A couple of them accompanied our last assignment home, and one more stayed there to take care of the office. It's just me and Olly left here in France."

I saw my chance to get to know him better, so I just asked, "Is Kannon always this grumpy?"

Sparrow eased onto the couch across from me. "There are shadows in him. But mostly he's a growly teddy bear. You just have to get to know his quirks and what makes him tick, I guess."

That seemed like an understatement. "It must be a full-time job trying to understand what makes the man tick."

She laughed. "True enough. But you know what? At the core, Kannon's one of the best people I know. He legitimately wants to help people. And these days, that's hard to come by."

I studied her. "You respect him a lot, don't you?"

She nodded. "Of course I do. He's— Well, he gave me a shot when no one else would. He's sharp as a tack, keeps the bullshit level low, and the company gave me a family. I'd like to think that I gave him the same thing."

I studied her closely. "Are you two—?"

Sparrow lifted a brow and gazed at me over the top of her laptop. It took her a moment to realize what I was asking, and then her brows lifted before she threw her head back with a loud bark of laughter. The action made her look young and beautiful, as if she didn't have a care in the world having to watch some random woman that people were shooting at. "Oh my God, that's priceless. I'm going to tell Olly."

A flush crept up my neck. "I'm sorry. That was really nosy. None of my business."

Sparrow put out a hand and waved me off. "No. No. Oh God, no. You can relax. It's not like that. It has *never* been like that. He's obviously very pretty. It actually became kind of a game to watch women throw themselves at him. We have running bets on the team as to how long he can ignore them before he actively brushes them off, or how long before he gives in. It depends. But no, it's never been like that with me and him. He's my boss. And my friend. And yes, surprisingly, over the course of the last few years, he has become family."

"How long have you been with him?"

She smiled then, and I realized what a travesty it was that she didn't smile more often. I'd guess she was in her late twenties, close to my age. But that smile, it lit up her whole face. It probably stunned men and women alike, turning them completely stupid. When she was stern, there was a glint in her eye that said, if crossed, she could be deadly. Which I respected. But she was gorgeous with her high cheekbones and thick dark waves cascading down her back. Not to mention the kind of lips women the world over probably tried to emulate.

"I'd been sacked from my government job, for something that was not exactly my fault. I'd been applying at places, but nothing was coming through, and things were getting a little desperate. Luckily, a friend of a friend asked him to give me a call, and he did. He saved my ass. That's Kannon for you. He comes through when you need him."

I nodded. "He seems like that kind of guy."

She still watched me, and I could feel her eyes dissecting every nuanced movement, the brush of my fingers through my hair, my lifted brow, the graze of teeth over my lip, and I was hyper aware of it all. "You're curious about him."

I shook my head. "I... Well, I am a mess, and I probably have no business asking anyone about their relationships, considering I don't really know how to maintain one."

She tilted her head, her gaze on my face. "Why is that?"

"My parents, when they were alive, they doted on me. I was the only girl. The youngest. Desperate to be seen. They poured love on me as much as they could. But they were busy, as active royals should be. So there were lots of nannies and governesses and boarding school and the like. I missed out on some things like the ability to climb into bed with my mom, chats about relationships, and someone to actually talk to." I shook my head. "I've always had my Aunt Rebecca, though she didn't fill that space completely. She did her best. Was always kind and *there* for me, even when trying to mold me into the princess I needed to be. It was her duty to ensure I was ready to be Princess London, not *just* London."

"That couldn't have been easy."

I smiled softly. "No, but it's hard to complain when there are so many others who have had horrible lives while I've been privileged with many parts of mine."

Sparrow studied my face. "You had your aunt, which I'm thankful for, but what about your brothers? Are you close to them?"

I looked down at my hands, trying to formulate my response. "As much as I love them, I've always felt a little separate from my brothers. I'm the last born after three sons. I knew my Mom wanted a daughter. My brother Roman got the bulk of the royal-duty role. Wilder is in intelligence, though he's also a lovely pianist. Breck... Breck is into tech and the like. You never know what he'll be up to next, but he's always had more freedom. And I am... I don't know. I've always sort of felt like the appendage. The jewel, as they called me. The Jewel of Alden. Not expected to say much or have opinions, or generally stand out in any way, I guess."

Sparrow's brows knitted. "But you're beautiful. And if you're off to the Amazon to take photos, you're probably talented. I guarantee you're probably well educated, so you're smart too."

"All of those are surface things. My parents loved me. I knew that. My brothers love me as well. I know that too. But I don't know. I've always felt like the forgotten one. Like for anyone to have any kind of deep connection with me just wasn't going to happen."

"That can't feel good. And it sounds like a lonely life."

I shrugged. "I don't need pity. My life is good. Better than so many others. I just always feel a little restless, you know? Disconnected. Always looking for that real connection point that anchors me."

"I know, of course. Everyone wants to feel like that. Everyone wants to have that thing that feels like it belongs to just them. Everyone wants to be seen and appreciated, right?"

"I just wish I could be appreciated for more than my womb."

Sparrow snorted. "I still can't believe they're trying to marry you off to get someone for a line of succession. It's ridiculous. What about love? And like a real, deep understanding of knowing someone? I mean, do you think your brothers are going to be able to just change the law?"

I sighed. "I don't really have much choice but to believe in them, right? And to believe in you guys to make sure someone doesn't kill me before they can get it done. I don't know. All my life, I haven't really been special. And I was okay with that. I've been looking for a real sense of purpose and grounding for a long time."

Sparrow nodded. "That's kind of how I felt when Kannon took me on. It was like all the years of not quite fitting in finally paid off, and suddenly I knew where I belonged."

"That's exactly it. You never really know. But soon, hopefully, I'll be able to get back to my life. Get back to work. Put all this behind me."

Sparrow smiled softly. "If anyone can make it happen, it's Kannon." She closed her laptop and watched me. "What is it that's going on between you and Kannon?"

My face flushed with heat. "You must be protective of him."

Sparrow smiled. "I am, but he's also a grown-ass man. However, I will tell you that even though I wasn't around when Phoebe died, I know it still sits with him. Some of the others were around, and they've told me that thing that he does, not letting anyone in, it used to be much, much worse. This is Kannon 2.0."

My brows popped. "You're kidding. It's like I'm talking to a brick wall."

"I will tell you though, I've never seen him this rigid and stubborn before. He's being a right pain in the ass."

That made me laugh. "Ugh, thank God. I thought it was just me. What have I ever done to him?"

"I don't know. I guess I'm saying don't lose faith or hope. He's a good guy."

I read between the lines of what she *wasn't* saying. "And you'd rather I didn't hurt him?"

She shrugged. "That too. He's the only family I've got. I don't need him moping around."

"I'm aware that he had a wife before, and he lost her. I'm not trying to mess with him. I'm just trying to figure out what the hell is happening to me and get back to my life."

She cocked her head. "Maybe it's none of my business, but I think you could be good for him."

I laughed at that. "Hardly. He probably needs someone a little more open. Someone who knows exactly who she is in the world and what she needs. I don't think I'm that person."

"Maybe you are exactly what he needs."

I just blinked at her. "Well, I guess we'll see about that."

"I guess we will."

I leaned closer, studying her face. "What about you? You said you and Kannon aren't a thing, but how about anyone else on the team? Olly's very attractive." It had been awhile since I'd had girl talk like this. Rian was even busier than I was, and while we talked nearly every day, I didn't have many friends back home, thanks to my position. I had Kate, and was forever grateful I did, but she couldn't always be there.

She gagged. "Oh my God, the boys are like my brothers. Where I worked before, it was a boys' club, and I was a moron and fell in love with my boss. You know, as one does. I could see the disaster coming. I just didn't duck and dive quickly enough, and I got hurt. I've put relationships on pause for a minute."

"There's nothing wrong with taking a beat. While I might not be one for love, I am very good at fixing people up." At least I thought I was. I hadn't heard any complaints from those at court and in my other life at work.

She laughed. "Oh no, I beg you. Please, I'm not really good at being fixed up."

"Oh come on, we could go trolling on the internet. Maybe next time you're in Paris, you can meet my friend Rian and we can all go out."

Sparrow grinned at that. "Now *that* I can get behind."

I smiled. "You know what's funny? Talking to you made me realize I haven't had a good girl chat in a million years. It's nice to have that again."

Sparrow grinned. "When Kannon said princess, I

thought we were getting, you know, a Kardashian or something."

I snorted a laugh. "I mean, don't get me wrong. I can bust it out if I have to."

She chuckled. "Please, no."

"A lot of people tell me I'm not what they expected, which is good, I guess, but it also makes me feel somehow lacking. It's nice to have a friend who isn't worried about trying to date one of my brothers or who is only hanging out with me because I can get them into some A-list parties. Being assigned to guard me, notwithstanding, I think I like you."

Sparrow grinned. "I think I like you too. You're not so bad for a princess."

"And you aren't so bad for a bodyguard. Now please, tell me what you like in a guy, or a girl. I can find you someone."

She laughed. "I'm not going to get out of this, am I?"

"Nope, and apparently, I've got nothing but time."

She flushed and ran a hand through her hair. "Okay, fine. I've got a list of requirements."

I laughed and closed down all of my work stuff. "Okay, how about we start with a Charlie Hunnam type and go from there."

"I do like how you think."

Chapter 14
LONDON

Cue the solo ballad

AFTER SPARROW LEFT, I RETURNED TO MY ROOM and sat in the middle of the bed, trying my best to put my thoughts together. I had to figure out a way to help my brothers nullify the succession law. I also needed to figure out exactly who had the most to gain, who was after me, and why.

Not to mention the fact that I still had to figure out how to get back into my boss's good graces. I'd had two opportunities and blown them both. When this mess was over, I wanted a life. A *real* one. And like it or not, Roman was going to have to give it to me.

All of that filtered through my mind, but they weren't the only thoughts I was wrestling with.

Not when Kannon echoed through my thoughts and made me think of things I needed that I couldn't have.

It had to be the emotions of everything else tumbling through my brain for me to feel like this.

I barely knew him, but I *felt* him. He had told me his deepest and darkest secrets, and he had leaned on me.

Maybe for him, it could be just sex. It could just be flesh and need and desire.

And I would have to be okay with that.

What worried me most was the idea that I kind of wanted more.

Could I fall for him?

No, I couldn't. That would put me in the lane of every single woman in history who had fallen for the man who had saved her life.

But I needed to save my own life. I needed a life that was mine, one that I had fought for, and could continue working on.

I had to focus on that and not on the idea that a man who touched me, who said he craved me, could want anything more.

Because going down that path would only hurt us both in the end.

But I wanted it. Wanted him. No man had ever

touched me like that. No man had ever made me feel like that.

This feeling, it couldn't be love.

Because if it was, then I had not only lost my mind, but I'd also lost all semblance of the person I tried so hard to be.

I got up from the bed and began to pace the room.

There were more important things in life than the emotions that I was going through. Focusing on those emotions kept me from concentrating on what was important. Like who was after me, who wanted to hurt my family.

Something nagged me in the back of my mind, something I needed to think of, but I couldn't pinpoint what it was. I was so out of my depth, and I needed to find my footing.

It wasn't easy when all I could do was close my eyes and imagine Kannon over me and me arching into him.

"And that's enough of that."

I ran my hands through my hair, picked up my camera, and went through a few of my photos. I flipped through the images, remembered the moment I'd stood in place to take each one.

I was the one capturing those memories, and yet I was on the other side of the lens. I was part of the moment, and yet not. That's how I felt in every other part of my life too, like I was there but not really an integral part of what was happening around me. Part of the royal family, just so far down the hierarchy that I was only there as a stand-in until Roman finally married.

I was part of my siblings' lives, and yet wasn't one of the brothers, and therefore always on the outside looking in.

I was part of my country, and yet mostly just a symbol for them.

I was part of the world, and yet apart. Watching, waiting, asking to be let in, knowing I would never be.

I couldn't take that step forward and push my way through, because if I did, it might irrevocably harm others around me.

Look at what had happened once I left the confines of my country. Bullets had come at me, but not *just* at me.

Kannon's team was in danger because they were protecting me.

How could I go into the real world and pretend that I could keep others safe?

The fact that those words echoed something Kannon had said didn't escape me.

Kannon.

The one man I couldn't have.

Not because he didn't have the right bloodlines. Not because my family wouldn't approve.

He was just as growly and grumbly as my brothers.

They would probably welcome him with open arms after they interrogated him and kicked him around a bit just for good measure.

Because that's what big brothers did.

But no, Kannon had loved before. He had been broken.

And he felt like all that was left was a shell. Though the shell that had been left behind wasn't substantial enough to venture far into the world. He was here to protect. He was there for others.

But not for himself.

And therefore, not for me.

There was a light knock on my door.

Assuming it was Sparrow, I called out, "Come in."

The door opened, and I set down my camera. My words caught in my throat as Kannon walked into the bedroom, his hands running a towel over his head, his body glistening with water from the shower.

I licked my lips and swallowed hard as my gaze trailed down his body, over his thick chest, his narrow hips. That little line of hair that went from his belly-button and disappeared below the waistband of his jeans.

He was barefoot, his feet sexy and tan.

He had left the button undone on his jeans, and they were open just enough that I knew he wasn't wearing any underwear, and the coarse hair that shadowed his cock was barely visible. The long, thick line of his erection bulged beneath the zipper, and I could see a very noticeable line that visibly grew at my heated attention.

I swallowed hard and licked my lips again, and Kannon let out a rough chuckle.

"Do you think you can pull your eyes off my cock long enough to meet my gaze?" Kannon asked, his voice deep.

I flushed.

His gaze raked over me just the same, and I knew he was picturing me naked.

After all, he had already seen and touched and tasted every inch of me.

Why shouldn't I enjoy the feast in front of me?

"We're not going to talk?"

I pinched the bridge of my nose. "Kannon, I—"

"Got what you wanted, so you took off?"

"That's not what happened, and you know that. I just needed to breathe, and I couldn't do that in your bed."

"So instead of talking to me, you bolted?"

He had a point. "I'm sorry. I just have no idea what I'm supposed to do right now. I've never been impulsive. I've never felt...anything like this before. I don't have any answers, and I have no idea what to do."

He lifted a brow. "I didn't think you'd tell me the truth."

"Well right now, it's all I have." I didn't like the way simply telling the truth made me feel bare.

"I'll tell you another truth. We want each other. And we're spinning out about what that means. It doesn't need to mean anything. I'm not going to ruin your life, and my life is already in ashes. But we can't seem to stay away from each other. While we're here, we stop fighting. It's fucking exhausting."

I swallowed hard. "I—I've never had a one-night stand before."

"And that's not what this is. Can you stay away from me? Or do you feel the pull right now?"

"I shifted on my feet and spoke the truth. "I feel it."

"Good. Me too. Now, do you want to keep fighting, or do you want to give in?"

"I—" God, for once in my life how good would it feel to not worry about doing what was expected? "I want you."

His gaze was molten lava on mine then he dropped the towel and shrugged so casually I nearly swooned.

Damn the man, using his sex appeal to cloud my thoughts.

I wasn't thinking clearly as it was, and he wasn't making it any easier.

He scratched his stomach, the motion making his arms flex and his pants ride just a little bit lower.

I could see the outline of the base of his cock, and my mouth watered.

Damn the man.

"You're just going to stand there and present yourself like a peacock?" I asked, enjoying the way that his eyes narrowed just a bit at my tone.

"I think you could be doing something far better with your mouth than using it to sass me."

"Sass? Is that what you call someone talking back to you?"

My heart fluttered in my chest. I was having too much fun. He helped me get my mind off everything else, and for that, I was grateful because it meant I could just live in the moment.

I needed to. I had never allowed myself that before. So for now, I would have fun. And when he had to walk away, I'd find a way to deal with it. After all, I'd done that already. Countless times when I'd been the one left behind.

I sauntered over to him, a smile on my lips and humor in my gaze as I slowly ran my fingers along the edge of his jeans.

His jaw tightened, and I heard the growl in his chest.

"You're playing with fire, princess."

"I think there's something else you want me to be playing with."

Then I went down on my knees in front of him.

"Jesus Christ, London." His voice went raw. "You don't have to do that."

I only had to unzip his zipper very carefully and then tug his pants down slightly, and his cock sprang free into my hand.

He was long, hard, and thick. My fingers couldn't even wrap around the base, and he groaned as I pumped him twice.

"I think you should stop telling me what to do," I said right before I pounced.

I laughed at him, angling my mouth. I hollowed my throat and bobbed, licking him, taking more. I let his balls fall heavily into my free hand and kept going.

When he tugged on my hair, I didn't pull back, and then he pressed me farther down onto him, fucking my face as he buried himself in me. I groaned, humming against him.

He pumped and then pulled hard, tugging me away.

I looked up at him and licked my swollen lips, and before I knew it, he was down on his knees in front of me. He sent a brazen kiss across my lips and tugged my hair even harder.

"I'm going to blow my load, and I'm not about to do that down your throat."

Somehow, I was on my back, my pants were off, and his head was between my legs.

I arched my back as he spread me, licking me, sucking. His tongue stretched me, eating me out as if he was a man dying of thirst and need.

I let my hands work themselves under my shirt, playing with my breasts as I arched my back. The tableau of his head between my legs nearly sent me over the edge.

And then, when he twisted his lips and hummed against my clit, I fell.

I came, jerking in his hold as he pressed my hips down, laughing at my orgasm.

Then he was over me, kissing me, his dick on my belly, hard and wet, and I ached for him.

I ran my fingernails down his back, digging into the skin, and he groaned, deepening the kiss.

And then he pulled away from me and tugged my shirt over my head, and then *his* hands were on my breasts, his lips plucking at my nipples.

"Kannon," I moaned.

"That's it, say my name."

"Inside me. I need you inside me."

"Need a condom," he whispered.

"Hurry. Please."

I never begged. A princess did not beg. But I would

fall to my knees and bow before his massive erection, even if it made me the worst of beggars.

Then he was back, the condom over his length, and he pushed me to all fours.

"That's it. I want to fuck you from behind. You want that, princess? You want your fingers in the carpet as I pound into you from behind?"

Over my shoulder, I scowled at him. "That's a lot of talking. Inside me. Now."

"Yes, Your Highness."

And then he gripped my hips and pounded into me in one thrust.

I froze, his fingers digging into me, my body stretching to accommodate his size.

"Jesus Christ, you're so tight. Jesus." He just kept muttering that over and over again, and then I pressed my ass against him, rotating gently. Needing him to move.

In that space, time stretched forever as I waited for him to make love to me. And then he did.

I lowered my head, my cheek to the carpet as he thrust in and out of me, pounding into me as if neither of us knew when to stop.

I met him thrust for thrust, my body aching, my need increasing with each movement.

He slid one hand around, flicking my clit, the other squeezing my breast before coming back to my hips.

My knees ached, and I knew I'd have rug burn in the morning, but if he kept hitting that spot, I really didn't care.

There'd be aches, and there'd likely be bruises, and it would all be absolutely worth it.

Because this was everything.

I grunted, shouting his name, and then he had me up again, my back to his front as he pounded in me, one hand around my throat, his fingers along my jaw, the other hand over my clit.

"There are other people in the house, princess. They'll hear you if you shout my name while you're riding my cock. You've got to be quiet. You don't want them to hear you. You don't want them to hear how much of a bad princess you are. How much you like taking my cock."

"Kannon," I whispered, the illicitness of it all turning me on even more.

If he had said anything like that outside of what we were doing just then, I'd have slapped him, kicked him in the balls, and told him exactly who I was. But right then? Hottest thing I'd ever experienced.

He flicked his finger over my clit again, turned me ever so slightly to capture my lips, and I came, my pussy clamping around his cock.

He filled me then, his entire body shaking as he

pounded into me one last time, the condom the only thing between us.

I fought to catch my breath, fought to catch everything.

Because I fell into the abyss with him, and I knew there would be no crawling out.

Not without pain. Not without forgetting.

But for now, it didn't matter.

For now, he was with me, and that was all that mattered.

I'd have to face the truth after he walked out.

And I would do that.

But for now, I could pretend.

For now, I could feel.

Chapter 15
KANNON

Mistakes happen. Life shouldn't be one of them.

I woke up slowly, not knowing where I was like I usually did. Years of training had taught me to open my eyes as soon as I woke up, assess my surroundings, get my bearings, and know what situation I was in. Now it wasn't like that.

Because of the woman in my arms.

The woman whose ass was currently pressed against my dick. I had come to talk to her for a reason. To do another security protocol for her next family call. To make sure she'd eaten something. I knew the stress could mess with appetite.

Shut up, you wanted to talk.

Which was such bullshit. I never wanted to talk. But I hated the chasm between us. Problem was I was there to protect her, not fuck her. Someone needed to tell my dick that, though.

Something lurched inside me at the word fuck and the emotion pulled my lips into a frown.

Why didn't I like the word *fuck* when it came to her? It shouldn't bother me. She couldn't be more than just a fuck. And yet, I couldn't get her out of my mind.

I wasn't a complete fool. I knew that outside of this house, this situation, we didn't work. She'd go home. And I'd go back to work. But for this moment in time, if I could chase the shadows from her eyes, I would.

What about your own?

She might not agree, but I cared about her. She didn't need my particular brand of bullshit. But If I could make her smile for a couple of days, then I'd do that and pray to Christ we didn't destroy each other in the end.

My hand was on her breast, and her nipple pebbled into my palm. She moved back into me in her sleep, as if needing my touch, and my cock pressed against her ass. One movement and I'd be able to slide right into her.

But hell, I couldn't.

Not when doing so would screw up what I was trying to stay away from to begin with. And I didn't have

CARRIE ANN RYAN & NANA MALONE

a condom, and there was no way I was going to slide into her sweet heat without protection. But Christ, the more I thought about it, the harder I became.

I slowly pulled away at that thought, knowing that I couldn't do this again. I needed to walk away and be the man that protected her and not let myself fall again.

Because I could feel it.

That unnamed emotion that wanted something more. I hadn't let myself feel that since Phoebe.

And I'd be damned if I let anyone that close again.

I slid out of bed then tucked London in, as if seeing her uncomfortable in any way did something to me that I'd rather not think about. No, it was just because I didn't want her to get a fucking cold.

Because if she did so, then I'd have to deal with her complaining. That was why I did it. Not for some sense of comfort or some other shit.

I headed to the bathroom, took care of business, and washed my hands, my gaze straying to the trashcan right next to the sink.

I frowned, trying to wrap my mind around what I was actually seeing.

"Jesus Christ," I muttered and then reached down into the trashcan, lifting away a piece of tissue and cursing.

"Fuck."

My heart raced, and I clenched my fist at my side,

knowing I couldn't go back and change it, but Jesus, how could this have happened?

No, it had to be a mistake. It had happened later, not during. It couldn't be this. It just couldn't.

"Jesus."

I'd tell her when she woke up. Then we'd figure out what to do. Because maybe the condom had broken after, not when I had been buried balls-deep inside her, both of us screaming each other's names while trying to keep quiet so the others couldn't hear.

Who are you kidding?

I damn well knew the others had heard, and I hadn't given a shit. That just egged me on even more. Just made me want to pound into her harder. But apparently all that pounding meant I'd fucking broken the condom. I tried to breathe, but I couldn't.

This was not fucking happening.

I quickly changed then headed back out to the bedroom where London was still sleeping. I didn't wake her, but as soon as I got back into the room after checking in with my team, I'd tell her.

Then we'd deal with it. *That's going to go well.*

I shook my head, pulling my gaze from her soft curves and the way that she looked so gentle and peaceful in her sleep.

As if she wasn't already scared shitless.

I found Olly and Sparrow in the dining room, going over plans and purposely not meeting my gaze.

Fuck, apparently, they *had* heard. We hadn't been quiet last night. London was a screamer.

"I need coffee," I muttered.

"Feeling a little parched there, boss?" Sparrow said.

I narrowed my gaze at her as she and Olly smirked right back.

"Fuck all y'all," I mumbled as they snickered.

I poured myself coffee and drank half the cup, ignoring the fact that it scalded my throat. Thankfully it wasn't too hot since they had left the coffee pot out, but Jesus, I really was a glutton for punishment.

"You okay, boss?" Sparrow asked, and I resisted the urge to flip her off.

"Fine," I muttered.

"Just curious. What with all the shouting and the praying to God," she said, buffing her nails.

"Stop it."

"Hey, we're not saying anything," Sparrow said, holding up her hands.

Olly, indeed, didn't say anything, but I noticed the look in his eyes.

"You're saying something right now."

"You're right. I am. I just want you to be smart. You know who she is, boss."

"I'm not going to fucking hurt her."

She shook her head, and I opened my mouth to snap back, but she held up her hand.

"I believe you. I believe you're going to try. But what about you? What happens when she hurts you?"

I frowned, shaking my head. "It's not... It's not that."

I thought about that broken condom, but I knew it was a long shot. I did not just get her pregnant the night before.

Just the thought of that word made me want to throw up, and I swallowed hard.

Because I had already nearly been a father once, had almost held my child, and now I couldn't. All of it was gone, and I wasn't going to put myself in that situation again.

"I'm going to go wake her up. We have shit to do."

"You've got it. We're here when you need us."

I shook my head and headed back to the room. London was up by then, already dressed and her hair piled on the top of her head. She frowned at me as I handed over a cup of coffee, and she studied my face.

"What's wrong? Is it about last night?" she asked, and I felt like a fucking bastard.

"Nothing's wrong," I muttered. My tone tight.

She flinched then rolled her shoulders back, becoming the strong princess I knew she was, strapping on that armor that she used to block out the rest of the world.

"I thought... You know what, never mind."

"There's something you need to know," I said, figuring I should just rip off the bandage quickly.

"Did you find out who it was?"

I shook my head. "We will. Today if I have anything to say about it." I paused, knowing I needed to tell her. "Hell, I'm pretty sure the condom broke last night."

Her face drained of color, and she set down her untouched coffee on the nightstand. "Are you sure?"

"Looks like it in the trash, but it could have happened afterward when I tossed it in. I'm pretty sure I would have noticed last night if it had happened during..."

Not that I had been thinking too hard other than wanting to get inside her the night before, but I didn't say that.

She let out a shuddering breath and once again rolled those shoulders back. "Okay. Fuck."

I hated the fact that my dick went hard at the sound of that word coming from her mouth.

"I don't know what you want to do about it," I said honestly. "It's your choice."

She shook her head. "I'm on birth control. I have been for as long as I was old enough to make my own decisions. But we can take other precautions."

I nodded. "We'll take care of that today."

"Good."

"Well then." I let out a breath, knowing what I was going to say was going to be the worst possible thing, but it was what was needed. "That can't happen again." I felt like I was shredding my heart. Last night was one thing, but nothing said get your house in order like a fucking broken condom.

"Excuse me?" she asked, taking a step back. "What the hell?"

"I'm just saying, this was a wakeup call. I'm your bodyguard, not someone you should be fucking."

"*Fucking*. So that's it?"

"That was always what it was going to be, princess."

"I hate when you call me that. You use it as an endearment once and then a slap in the face the next time. Make up your fucking mind."

"Look at you with the potty mouth. Is that what happens when you fuck the help?" If I made her angry enough, she'd stay away. She'd see how bad I was for her.

"You're lucky I don't slap you right now."

"Maybe you should just do it and get it over with," I dared her. I sat my coffee down before I spilled it or broke the fucking mug. "You and me? Last night I—" I needed to get this right. "I thought we could keep this contained here. That I could give you what you needed for a moment in time. But this morning, that was one hell of a wakeup call. You're not some

CARRIE ANN RYAN & NANA MALONE

random woman. You're a princess. It will be bad for you."

"Fine." She squared her shoulders. "But you know what? I've had just about enough of men making decisions for me. You're scared. Say that. Don't give me some bullshit about not being right for me. About *us* never working..."

"I'm not scared of anything," I lied.

"And you are an idiot if you believe that."

"Maybe I am, but it doesn't matter. You're not for me just like I'm not for you. You're a fucking princess, or did you forget that? Guys like me don't end up with the happily ever after. That's not how this goes."

"How can I forget it? Everyone reminds me every second that they possibly can. And when I look in the mirror, I see the tiara even if it's not on my head. I had to leave my country because of the title I have. Because of rules that I had no part of, rules I didn't even realize existed that want to change my purpose and put me on a path that I didn't ask for. I know I'm a princess, Kannon."

"And I'm not your fucking prince. You belong with your family, and we'll get you back there. I'm just the farm boy, and nothing is as you wish."

I let out a curse as she pushed past me, the look in her gaze pure hatred. She shoved her shoulder into my side and kept going, but I could see the tears that were beginning to fall.

I had done that. I had hurt her. And I deserved whatever came next.

I let out a couple of breaths, knowing I just needed to calm down. But I couldn't. Not when I had fucking hurt her. I knew I couldn't be with her. It wasn't smart for either of us. But what I could do was not hurt her anymore.

I didn't have to push her away because she was going leave anyway. I didn't have to hurt her to accomplish that.

She'd realize who I was, and then she'd walk away. I had simply done it first.

"Fuck," I whispered.

I pushed out of the room and looked around the house. My team was gone. They must be switching out patrols, and I was fine with that.

But where the hell had London gone?

Something was wrong, I thought, the hairs on the back of my neck tingling. I frowned, went out the door, and everything inside me went on alert. There was a large pool of blood around the poolside cabanas, and neither London nor Sparrow was anywhere to be found.

Someone had fucking taken them.

And it was all my fucking fault.

Chapter 16
LONDON

The ones you never saw coming hurt the most.

I AWOKE TO WHAT FELT LIKE A MOUTH FULL OF cotton. My head throbbed and my muscles ached. I tried to blink, but my eyelids were far too heavy. When I tried to raise my hands to rub them, the skin on my wrists felt abraded.

What the hell?

And then in startling clarity, it all came back in a panorama of images just like in a movie. I'd been angry with Kannon. Angry that he'd pushed me away. Angry that he hadn't wanted me. And then I'd gone running from the house. It was like every other day, but the security gates were open, and Olly... Where had Olly been?

That's right. Kannon had said he'd gone for supplies. Had he not reset the alarm? That didn't even make sense. They were all so careful. These three people I didn't know had decided to protect me, even though they had other things to do, lives to get back to, and I'd put them in danger.

Oh shit. Sparrow.

I'd stormed out of the house, eager to just get some space. I went out and around to one of the guest houses. I figured she could help me with her boss a little bit. And I found her by the pool under one of the cabanas.

Everything started coming back at once. There was a horrendous sticky substance on the tiles near the pool, and her silky dark hair had been matted with it. *Oh God,* this was my fault. Someone had come to that house looking for me. Instead, they'd found Sparrow, and they'd hurt her. I'd been so preoccupied with my damn love life I hadn't even noticed her until it had been too late. There wasn't even time for me to run or scream or do something, anything. I just stood there, staring at her. The woman had become my friend, and I had been unable to help her. *Is she going to be okay?*

"Uh-uh-uh, I wouldn't do that if I were you. The more you struggle, the more the restraints are going to chafe." I forced my eyes open then, turning toward the voice. *That voice*, it was all too familiar. It was only then that I realized I was on a plane. A private one. My hands were pinned with zip ties to the seat, and my Aunt Rebecca was lounging on the seat across from mine. "Yes, darling. You never were particularly bright, were you?"

I frowned, trying to understand what the hell was going on. This was my aunt. My safe harbor. The one who'd been there for me after my parents died when I had no one else. *Why was she doing this?* "Where is my friend? Where is Sparrow?"

"You can stop with that face. Like this is some grand betrayal. And the other woman is being dealt with. Shame she had to get caught up in all of this."

I tried to form words, but my mouth was having a hard time working around my thoughts. Finally, I managed to mutter, "Why?"

"Sweetheart." She leaned forward, placing her elbows on her knees and clasping her hands together. I'd never seen her look so free. Her hair was down and loose for once, not pinned back in an elegant chignon or styled in some up-do that was "befitting her age" as she liked to say. Instead it was down and hung around her shoulders. It made her look younger, less matronly, softer. And she had on makeup. Not the usual understated nude lipstick she wore, but bright flamenco red. And she was in a turquoise pantsuit.

She looked ready for battle in the boardroom. "Don't worry your pretty little head about these things. There are events happening here that are way above your pay grade."

"I trusted you."

We all had. Bile filled my throat as I desperately tried to catch up. This woman...this was my aunt? She'd been part of all of this? Oh God, she'd hurt Sparrow.

How had I missed it?

How had we *all* missed it?

"Well, that was your first error. God, how many times you cried on my shoulder. 'Oh auntie, my life is so hard. Nobody loves me.' Do you have any idea how many times I wanted to tell you what a whiny little brat you were being? You wanted Mommy and Daddy back to tell you how loved you were, and yes, that you too could be special. The thing is, you're not. You're a tool. And, had everything gone as planned, I would have used you appropriately. But you and your brothers had to entertain other ideas. This has always been your problem. You're far too independent."

Who the hell was this woman? "No, this isn't right. This isn't you. You don't even have anything to gain by kidnapping me. Why?" It didn't make any sense. Aunt Rebecca would gain *nothing* from my death.

"Well, you see, love, I never meant to kidnap you. You were supposed to have a little accident on the road, but the men I hired failed to successfully make that happen. Because, of course, poor, sweet, naïve, unloved London would find somebody who couldn't help but save her. Your knight in shining armor ruined every-thing. What is it about young pretty little things? Men cannot help but be drawn to you, to help you out of whatever peril you found yourself in. God, to be young again."

"You sound like you hate me." My hands shook, and even as I tried to get myself out of my restraints, I knew my aunt had been correct. Every time I moved, the bands went tighter, digging into my skin.

How was I going to get out of this?

I couldn't rely on anyone else. I needed to get to safety... But how?

"I do. But rest assured it's not anything that you've done to me *personally*. I can't have you going to your grave thinking 'Oh, how could I have wronged my beloved Aunt Rebecca?'"

I narrowed my gaze at her. "What I'm thinking is more along the lines of 'I can't believe Aunt Rebecca is such a cunt.'"

Her brows lifted, and I thought she was going to shoot me or have someone come out and just stab me or something, but instead, she laughed. "Oh my, look who's got teeth. Well, good for you. I always hoped that you would turn out more like me in the end."

I swallowed, trying to get some moisture in my mouth. "So I was supposed to have an accident, but now you've kidnapped me? What's the next part of the plan?"

"Listen to you talking about a next plan. I mean, how did you manage to find a security consultant, in Paris nonetheless?"

"Good things come to those who are nearly assassinated by their aunts."

She waved a hand and *tsked*. When she sat back, she gave me an easy smile. "Relax, we're going home. You will die in Alden, my love. Now, we'll have to stage it so that it appears you returned home unbeknownst to Roman, Breck, and Wilder. You thought you were going to fix your little predicament, and then you had an unfortunate accident there. Which is fine. I'll pick a narrative."

"You're crazy." I knew of course that you should never call a crazy person crazy, but sometimes you had to call a spade, a spade.

"No, I'm not crazy. You think you're the only one who has ever wanted anything in her life? You're the only one who's ever fought for anything? See, with the freedom you were given, all you wanted was someone to notice you and to love you. In my generation, before the laws were different, I couldn't even date unless my husband had passed away. And after your father died, well, I couldn't take the throne. All I could do was be an adviser to the young upstart. If he'd been underage, I could have ruled and set things up nicely for myself. But oh no, I had to be content to stay on the sidelines watching children lead *my* country, *my* home."

"That means what? You're trying to steal it to give it to Barkley? He'd just as soon ruin Alden and you in a breath. He'd be wasted most of the time. High too."

"No, he will fall in line, or I will remind him that there is a codicil that states should the ruler be determined to be unfit, and ruled so by the Council of Lords, that a regent will be appointed over him. As he's my son, I will rule."

I blinked at her, my heart racing as I tried to catch up. "My God, so this is what crazy looks like. I've always wondered."

She pushed to her feet and strolled over to me, placing her hands in her pockets. I tilted my chin up to glare at her. Even though she had the upper hand and the higher ground, I still gave her my best evil-death glare. "So, why lie? Why pretend?"

"Because this has been in the works for a very long time. At the very least, I was hoping to influence the court with your marriage, but you always seem to thwart my attempts. I could have ruled through you, and I'd have had those men's balls in a vice. Only every young man I introduced you to, you found something wrong with him. You were never satisfied. You always wanted more. You never wanted to be a princess. Over the years, do you understand how frustrating it has been? If you had just done as I told you, things would be easier now."

"Well, it's never going to happen now."

"You're right. It's not. Don't take it personally. I did care for you." She looked at her nails rather than my face as she said it.

"Oh yes, of course." I shook my left wrist. "These restraints prove that."

"Don't be mouthy. No one likes that in a woman."

"You know what's weird? In the last three days, I have learned more about love and connection than I have ever known. My brothers love me, but you kept me separated from them most of the time. And you did that on purpose, so I wouldn't know how much they loved me. I could hate you for that alone."

She snorted. "Oh sweetheart, look at you having opinions and thoughts all on your own, not ones that were given to you."

My hands shook. "I always had these thoughts. I felt sorry for you. You had no one to love you, so I made that my job. Too bad. But now that I see you clearly, I find you lacking."

Over the years, I'd learned to read Aunt Rebecca's rage button. It was in the corner of her mouth, the way it pressed ever so tightly when she was furious, even if only for just a second. Like the time Wilder had broken her priceless Ming vase, one that she'd acquired with her own money after Uncle George had died. She had been furious. Part of me thought that she would actually hit him or something, although, given what was going on now, that possibility probably hadn't been too far off.

I needed to get away, and if making her talk long enough so I could form a plan would work, I'd keep going. "Look, Aunt Rebecca, I know you've had a sad, sad life. You didn't get to rule like you thought you should. Too bad. But doing all of this is not going to change who you are inside. It won't make you any less miserable. You've believed that you were unlovable your whole life, and well, you've proven it now."

I didn't see it coming, didn't anticipate it and couldn't brace for it. And the sharp blow she dealt me exploded like a bomb inside my head and sent the edges of my vision graying as I once again slumped forward on my seat.

Chapter 17
KANNON

I never expected her.

MY HEART WAS DOING ITS LEVEL BEST TO JUMP outside of my body.

You idiot. You sent her out running away from you. And now she's gone.

My hands gripped the steering wheel tighter as I peeled out onto the main road. Next to me, Olly clutched at the door handle. "Jesus fucking Christ, boss, I thought the goal was to save Sparrow and London, not die on the way there."

I shot him a withering glance. "You have something else to say?"

CARRIE ANN RYAN & NANA MALONE

As one hand death-gripped the door and the other clutched his laptop, he shook his head. "Nope. Carry on."

I held back a snarl. "Where is her beacon?"

"It's stopped right now." He frowned as he peered closer. "Looks like it's headed toward the airport."

"If they're headed to the airport, they must have some big plans in place." This scheme had been well thought out, or at least sufficient enough to get by us. Damn it.

"I don't know. But judging by the blood we found by the pool house, one of them is in nasty shape. Either that or Sparrow took a piece of someone's ass. But if she was okay, she would have radioed in. The blood has to belong to one of them. Wherever the hell she is, we need to fucking find her soon. There was too much blood there, Kannon."

My heart continued to hammer. The spike of adrenaline that was normally a boon in times of crisis was instead making my head feel cloudy and foggy, and I had that brassy taste of fear and worry in my mouth.

I knew that taste well. It was the same one I'd had when Phoebe was murdered.

Is that going to help right now?

No, it wasn't going to help.

What *would* help was getting to her as fast as possible. And when we did, I would grovel the shit out of this. I'd fucked up. Pulling away had been the wrong move. Making her think I didn't want her had been absolutely the wrong move. I'd hurt her, and it was a move I could have killed myself for.

I wanted a chance to fix it, but I had to find her first.

Olly was busy in the passenger seat as he alternated between making sure that London's tracker hadn't moved and checking weapons. At his feet were boxes of ammo and our vests. I watched as he methodically clipped in ammunition, checked magazines, and made sure our vests were fully loaded with everything we would need for a small arsenal. I didn't know how many men we were going to face or who exactly had taken her, but I made a call to some friends of mine that had a security firm in New York. They had international agents, and I put out the SOS and asked if they had anyone close by to please send them in.

"Has the beacon moved?"

Olly's voice was quiet. "No. They've stopped. Looks like they are at Le Bourget Airport for private planes."

My hands worked the steering wheel, sliding back and forth, and back and forth. It didn't make any fucking sense. Why the hell would someone not just kill her where she was? Why not leave Sparrow behind?

Olly was obviously running those same questions

through his mind. "Doesn't something bother you about all of this?"

I lifted my brow. "What do you mean?"

He frowned at me. "None of this shit makes any sense."

"We're on the same path, Olly. For starters, it's like London fell into my lap, literally. And if I hadn't seen someone try and kill her with my own two eyes, I'd take this whole situation with a good dose of skepticism. I know she doesn't want us to look at her brothers, and honestly, they have nothing to gain if she dies. If this law goes into effect, her brother, the king, loses everything. But they are the only ones who knew where she was going."

Olly nodded. "The problem is that everything I was able to find on the family, including details about the obscure law, seems to prove they didn't know anything about it until recently as there have been zero moves on their part to stop it from happening. Including the king. He's been the damn monarch for years. Plenty of time to make an heir, unless he can't. Then there are the other brothers, one of whom obviously has been in the press a lot, Breck. I'm surprised he doesn't have any children anywhere, but currently, there are none we're aware of. If they *are* responsible for this, it makes no sense they'd let her leave the country in the first place."

"That's exactly it. There must be something we're missing."

Olly shrugged. "Unless they needed it to look like an accident. You said you found her in a ravine on the side of the road, right? And then, when you pulled her out, another car came by, basically attempting to finish the job?"

"What are you getting at?"

"Maybe whoever is doing this needs it to look like an accident."

I frowned at that. "So what? Did you find anything in that law that indicated that assassinations would change the requirements?"

He frowned, then tapped several more keys. "Not in so many words. But there is something vague about limitations on royals who commit crimes. It doesn't say what kind of crimes, but anyone convicted of committing those certain acts will lose their place in the line of succession."

I frowned at that. "So that was probably put in place to keep people from assassinating a king's new bride or basically, killing everyone off to move the royal line over a branch or two on the family tree. And London has got three older brothers, and it would be even harder to kill three additional people. Their parents died, but that was thirteen years ago. Anyone else who might have a claim to the throne, which would primarily be her aunt—"

Olly shook his head. "Actually, no. Her aunt is too old. No new monarch can be coronated if their age is over sixty. If you're sixty while you're on the throne, fair enough. You'll stay for as long as you want or until you die. But the line will automatically go to the next eligible heir in this case because the aunt is over sixty and she's not currently sitting on the throne. So that leaves out the aunt."

"Christ."

He typed on his keyboard some more. "That just leaves London's cousin, Barkley, as next in line. From what I can tell, he's a grade-A douche. Like the biggest, laziest kind of douchebag you can find. Drugs. Alcohol. Women. But he'll be king if this law is followed."

"At the very least, that's an incentive to get London to marry, not to kill her."

"Again, they let her run. They *helped* her run. That doesn't make any sense. They would lose their only chance of keeping the throne. And this guy Barkley would make King Joffrey look like a grandmotherly saint."

I frowned as my brain worked through it all. "Does it say anything about what happens to the monarch if he's deemed unfit?"

Olly was silent for a moment before he spoke. "Actually, if a monarch is deemed unfit by the Council of Lords, a regent will be placed over that monarch. And get this, no age restriction applies to the regent."

I cursed under my breath. *London's fucking aunt.* The one who'd kept these laws secret until the very last moment. The one London had sworn had only ever been loving and kind to her. I couldn't help but feel the need to throttle that woman's neck. She'd taken a vulnerable young girl like London and lied to her, manipulated her. For that alone, the old lady had to die.

"Man, this is full of shit."

With another sharp turn and a screech of my tires, I took a hard left toward the airport. I had to get to her before her aunt hurt her. Before her aunt broke her heart.

At the landing strip, I parked my car with another squeal of the tires, and then Olly and I bolted out of the car. He tossed me my vest and weapons, and as I palmed my Sig, I double-checked my com unit. Then we headed to the left.

"You check that building. I'll check the plane and make sure she's not on it."

"Roger that."

I rounded the side of the building. There were no cars. I saw a few people milling about inside, so I plastered myself to the side of the building using only quick short peeks to see inside before ducking under the sill and then sneaking around to the back. I jogged the hundred meters to the fence and onto the tarmac. Two people were milling around what looked like luggage carriers. I ducked behind one. Out of the corner of my eye, I saw Olly duck behind another and check it for signs of Sparrow in case they were leaving her behind. I checked my phone and saw that London's beacon was still on that plane.

Instead of running, I eased out from around the luggage carrier, nonchalantly walking toward the plane like I belonged there.

A guy with a clipboard was checking something. He looked up when he saw me. "Can I help you?"

He didn't seem to notice my vest or concealed weapons for what they were. "I need to speak to the lady on the plane."

He shook his head. "She's indisposed at the moment. She said no interruptions."

He clearly didn't mean London. "Sorry but it's urgent."

I made to bypass him, and he slapped a hand on my chest. His brows furrowed. "I told you, she just said not to interrupt her."

"And I told you it's urgent." I applied pressure at his pinky and right over his thumb, then twisted his hand up with mine, making sure that my knuckle hit that joint in his wrist. He immediately released me, wincing.

"What the fuck—?"

I applied more pressure and he fell to his knees. This time, he dropped the clipboard and reached for something at his lower back.

"I really wish you hadn't done that." Then my other hand delivered a hook shot which made him stumble back, and I launched myself at him. The easiest grasp points were his ears. As my knees hit his chest, he fell over, and I grabbed his ears, pulled forward once, and shoved back again with a hard slam on the gravel. He groaned, and his hand released whatever he was holding.

A quick glance down told me he wasn't done.

"I told you not to do that."

He was only injured, not dead. But if he was working for who I thought he was working for, he certainly deserved to be.

Turning him over, I used zip ties to secure his hands then grabbed one of the bandanas from my back pocket and shoved it into his mouth so he couldn't call for help. Then, as a final precaution, I grabbed him by the back of his shirt, dragging him with me and rolling him under the plane so if someone came by, they wouldn't see him right away. Then I palmed my weapon again and took the stairs two at a time.

Gently, I eased a foot inside and peeked in. No pilot. No guard. Just a woman in a blue-green pantsuit standing over someone slumped over one of the seats. I clicked the safety of my gun. "Back away, old lady."

The woman whirled around. Her hair was a dark auburn cascading over her shoulders. The funny thing was she had London's eyes, but unlike London's, there was no kindness in them. There was no love. They were cold and flat and dead. She must have been a hell of an actor to have played the family like she did.

"Oh, you're the commoner she hooked up with. Darling, I must say, this is very noble of you to come and try to save someone who has nothing to do with your paltry little life, but you miscalculated."

I heard a click behind me, and my heart nearly exploded. I'd been so focused on her that I hadn't heard the person behind me. Or maybe he was just as well-trained as I was and moved silently like the night.

"Drop the gun, asshole."

It was the last thing on earth I wanted to do.

"I will as soon as your boss lets me see if London is alive."

He pressed the gun to the small of my back. "You don't have a leg to stand on. Drop it."

He was right. I had no choice. I dropped the weapon as he requested just as London started to come to. She lifted her head. Her lids flickered, and then her eyes went wide as her gaze met mine. "Kannon?"

"Hey, princess."

"You came for me."

"Always."

The one with the auburn hair, I assumed she was London's aunt, rolled her eyes. "Oh my God, young love. Or maybe it's just my little niece spreading her thighs and falling for the nearest beggar she could find. London, say goodbye to your boyfriend. He really has become quite the thorn in my side. If it hadn't been for this idiot, you would have had a more peaceful death. You know, an accident along the side of the road. But he just had to come and save the day, the perfect white knight. Which now means your death will be more painful. I could torture you by holding you until I can find just the right moment and watch you die at home where your brothers will mourn you and your idiocy."

London lifted her gaze to her aunt. "You won't get away with this."

"Oh, sweetheart, I already have."

Outside the window, I saw Olly on one of the luggage carriers, stopping to look down at a bundle.

He'd found Sparrow.

Jesus fucking Christ.

Unfortunately, whoever had the gun in my back also noticed him.

"He brought a friend."

London's aunt glanced around. "Where?"

In that moment, the man behind me made the error of indicating toward the window, and that gave me my way in.

In the tight confines of the aisle, I spun into his arm with my hand and braced at my hip to catch his firing arm. I delivered an elbow to his temple and lifted his gun hand up to keep him from shooting at London. I brought my right arm down and placed it across his trachea, adjusting my grip on his wrist. I'd underestimated though.

He had a gun in one hand and a knife in the other. He managed to slice down at my arm before I braced my right hand on the shoulder of his suit, then brought him down hard on my knee. Fire raced up my arm, but I didn't let up.

I levered my arm back so it acted like a bar across his neck again, applied pressure, and he coughed. Then I brought him down with another harsh tug to my knee. He dropped the gun and the knife. He stayed down as he moaned. I used that opportunity to grab his ears and brought his face to my knee again.

London's Aunt Rebecca dove for the gun, but I reached it first, aiming it at her. "Uh-uh, you don't want to do that."

Rebecca scowled at me. "Why couldn't you just

leave her in that ravine? None of us would be here now."

"Sometimes the good guys win. Release her. Now."

I reached for the pliers inside the tool pocket of my vest and tossed them on the floor. "Now, no funny business. I promise you that I am a perfect shot."

For a moment, it looked like she wanted to argue with me. Then she did as she was told, first snipping the plastic zip tie at one of London's wrists and then the other. She held her hands up. "Happy?"

"What do you think? Put down the pliers, please."

She looked like she might want to jab London in the eye with them, but she didn't get the opportunity. London pushed to her feet, and with an open palm, she slammed her hand straight into her aunt's nose.

The older woman staggered back and howled. "What? How dare you?"

"You're lucky I didn't use a closed fist. You forgot Breck and Wilder taught me how to fight."

London staggered on her feet, but I held her steady as Rebecca tried to gain her footing. Blood spurted out of her nose, leaving vermillion spots on the pristine turquoise jacket of her suit. "Why couldn't you just do as you were told, London?"

London straightened her shoulders. "And why couldn't you not be a bitch?"

I eased forward with the zip ties, rolled Rebecca

CARRIE ANN RYAN & NANA MALONE

over, and then tied her wrists together. Then I lifted her gently and placed her on one of the seats. It was only then that I turned my whole attention to London. She was shaking on her feet, and I held her to me. "You're okay. You're okay."

"Oh my God, Sparrow. They hurt Sparrow. I think they brought her with us, but I don't know where she is, and—"

"It's okay. Olly has her."

"How did you know where to even find me?'

"One of the shoes that Sparrow brought you, there was a tracker in it."

She pulled back and blinked at me. "Wait, the same trick that whoever was following me used, you used that on me?"

I shrugged. "It's effective. No one ever checks the shoes."

She chaffed out a breath and tried to pull back from me, but I held tight. "I was so scared when I realized you were gone. I was terrified."

"We don't have to do this now, Kannon. I'm just—I just want to sleep."

I eased her back and ran my hands over her hair, tucking several wayward strands behind her ear. "I know. I just want you to know I love you. I'm sorry. I shouldn't have said what I said. The truth is I am scared to death. I met you only days ago, not even a week, and to already feel this way is terrifying to say the least. I should have never let you walk out. The last thing I want is to let you go."

Sobbing, she sank into me, and I held her, vowing to myself that I would do everything in my power to keep her close.

Chapter 18
KANNON

Running away is the best chance to survive.

I WOULD NEVER BE ABLE TO GET THE SIGHT OF London, hurt and looking so fucking scared, out of my mind.

Until the end of my days, the sound of her voice as she'd almost been killed would forever be entwined with that of Phoebe's.

I had lost my wife, my unborn child, and I had almost lost London.

I hated that feeling, like I was the common denominator. I was the one who hadn't been strong enough to protect Phoebe, to protect our child. And I'd nearly not been strong enough to protect London.

My hands fisted as I waited for Olly to finish working on my arm. It was a nasty slice, but I'd live. Sparrow had fought like the champ she was. She had a knot on the back of her head and some cuts and bruises from the scuffle by the cabanas. But the blood we'd found wasn't all hers. She'd managed to stab one of the men who'd taken her and London, but had taken a knife to the side. Thankfully it hadn't hit any major organs.

Olly nodded down at me. "Okay, boss, you should probably go see a doctor, but I know you want to get your girl home first."

I looked up at Olly and narrowed my eyes. "She's not my girl."

"Funny how usually the first thing out of your mouth is you don't need a damn doctor, but this time it's about the girl."

"You're lucky I like you, or I'd kick your ass right now."

"Kannon, you're bruised, bloody, and I'm pretty sure Sparrow could kick your ass."

"I heard that," Sparrow yelled from the other side of the room.

"Are you done?" I asked.

"I am. You can go see your... You can go see the princess," Olly backtracked.

I ignored him, nodded, and got up, wincing as I pulled on the bandage.

I'd been lucky. I knew that, but it still didn't mean I enjoyed bleeding like a stuck pig.

I'd go to the doctor if I felt like it, but most likely, I'd deal with it on my own like I always did. Today hadn't been the first time I'd been stabbed or shot, and sadly, it probably wouldn't be the last.

My job was dangerous. That meant I always needed to be on top of things. I hadn't been recently, and I knew exactly why.

London sat on a bench, her eyes wide, her face pale, and her whole body wrapped in a blanket.

The minute she spotted me, she stood up, pushed past Olly and the others, and came to me. She stopped right in front of me but didn't reach out to hold me, and I didn't know whether I was happy about that or disappointed. The indecision told me that what I was going to do later was the right thing.

"You're okay," she whispered.

"I am."

"Good. I can't believe.... I can't believe all that just happened."

I couldn't either, but I wasn't going to focus on that. I couldn't.

"You're fine. We're going to get you home. Your brothers have sent a plane."

Her voice was soft when she asked, "They did?"

"Their baby sister was kidnapped and almost killed. They want you home, London."

I heard the bitterness in my tone, and I felt more than saw the reproachful looks from Olly and Sparrow, but I ignored it.

I was so fucking scared, so worried about everything that just happened. And I didn't want to have to deal with it. I needed to get in and get out, just to make sure London was in safe hands.

"We need to head out."

There were others all around us, and I knew she wanted to say something, but I couldn't let her.

We needed to go. In hindsight, I suppose the longer I was with her, the more I wanted to stay. And I couldn't.

She needed to go home to her family. She needed to be a princess and a royal. And I needed to go back to what I was good at.

Protecting, killing, and bleeding.

None of which would work with London's life.

"Kannon, can we talk about what just happened?"

I looked at her then over at my team. "Olly, come on, let's go."

"Kannon."

I ignored London and turned, knowing that she

would follow because there was nowhere else for her to go.

We got into the SUV and headed toward the hangar where a private plane would be waiting to take her home, to her world that was far away from mine.

A private plane, royal galas, everything that wasn't part of my life.

She sat next to me in the back seat as Olly drove us. My arm was in a sling, so I couldn't do it myself. I just gritted my teeth and told myself we would get through this quickly, and then I could get on with my life and get away from London.

"Is your head okay?" I asked, breaking the silence I longed to keep.

She turned to me and swallowed hard. "I'm okay. I have a mild concussion, but they don't know if it occurred during the initial accident or now."

"You also have a few lacerations and abrasions," I said, ignoring her words. Because I needed to scream, shout, punch something.

Someone had dared to hurt her.

And I wanted blood.

But I couldn't have it. I had to walk away from the situation and let others handle it. As soon as I returned her to her brothers, London would no longer be mine to protect. When that happened, that meant everything between us was done.

That meant never seeing her again.

And that would be for the best.

It would just be a memory, a blip.

She was only a client.

I swallowed the lie. She looked at me as if she didn't understand me.

Hell, I didn't understand myself.

"What is wrong with you?" she asked, her voice low.

"Nothing, princess. We're getting you to safety. That's the job."

I heard Olly mumble under his breath, but I ignored him. I didn't care that I was the asshole here. The more of a dick I was, the easier she would be able to walk away. And that would be best for both of us.

We pulled into the hangar, and Olly went out to ensure everything was still safe. We might've caught her kidnapper and those who had helped Rebecca make plans, but it was never a good idea to let your guard down. Others could be there, waiting.

There could been a second conspirator in play.

I slid out of the car and went around to the other side to open the door for London.

I held out a hand, and she met my gaze, searching

for something. I didn't want her to see anything, so I lowered my brow and glared.

She glared right back, the look that I both wanted and hated all twisted into one.

"Come on, I'll get you to the plane."

"And then your job is done," she said flatly, sliding her hand into my free one. I helped her out of the SUV and then nodded at Olly to back away. I needed to tell her a few things, and it would already hurt her enough. We didn't need an audience for this. I at least owed her some privacy.

"I want to thank you," she said quickly, pulling my gaze to her.

She had a bruise under her eye and another one welling on her forehead.

Someone had marred her skin, had hurt her.

And I hadn't been strong enough to stop it.

You love her.

I did. And I hated myself for loving her. For loving anyone other than Phoebe.

I wasn't the right one for her anyway. She had a whole life outside of this one moment. A life where she had responsibilities and royal duties that had nothing to do with me. I was just the man she had leaned on in a time of need and the one she needed to walk away from now that it was over.

"No need to thank me. It was my job."

"You're acting cold again," she said softly. "I'm so sorry you were hurt because of me."

"Stop right there. None of this was your fault."

"Some of it was. I didn't see Aunt Rebecca for who she really is."

"You're right. You didn't. But people hide their true intentions all the time. It's not our fault if we can't see beneath every single layer."

Who was I talking to, her or me?

"What are we going to do now?" she asked, and I shook my head.

"You are going to get on that plane, and you are going to be safe in your life. No one's going to hurt you again."

I'd make that vow, even if I wouldn't be the one protecting her.

"And you expect me to just walk away?"

"You're safe now. I got you to the plane. My job is done."

She blanched but shook her head. "I love you, Kannon. Please don't go."

Her words were like a vicious knife sliced into my flesh, but I ignored them. They couldn't be real. She was just in shock.

"It's the best thing for you. You'll realize that soon enough."

She shook her head stubbornly. "You don't get to tell

me how I feel. I know it's crazy, it's too soon. But I know what I feel. We can work it out. I've never stood up for anything that I've wanted. I've always done what I was *supposed* to. And what did it get me? The one person I thought I could truly trust hurting me. So you're going to listen to what I feel, what I want. And that's *you*. We'll work it out somehow, Kannon, but don't let me go alone. Come with me. Let's find a way."

I didn't say anything. I couldn't.

I wanted to get on that plane, but I couldn't.

She wasn't mine. And that was something we both had to get through our skulls.

"You've got a life you need to lead. And I'm not part of it." I paused, the words tearing from me. "If something changes in the next month, you let me know." I didn't need to elaborate, the look in her eye told me she knew I was referring to the broken condom.

Hell, I didn't know what I wanted to come from that, but I knew what I needed.

"The job is done, ma'am."

She gripped my arm. "Kannon, if you do this, it's over. You don't get to break me again."

"Goodbye, Your Highness."

I expected her to hit me. To push at me. To shout. I turned on my heel, but she didn't follow. She stood there, so I met Olly's gaze on the other side of the space and nodded.

I knew she would be safe once I walked away, so I did. I left, knowing she was standing there, knowing she was breaking. But it only made sense. Because I was breaking right alongside her.

She wasn't mine, and she was only going to be a memory.

That was all that mattered.

Because as long as she wasn't near me, she would be safe, and she wouldn't have to think about who we could have been. And neither would I.

I walked away, leaving a part of myself behind and knowing I didn't want it back.

I had fallen again. I had made a grave mistake.

And now I would have to deal with the consequences.

Chapter 19
LONDON

Sometimes you need your girls.

One week later...

"I leave you alone for two days in my house, and the next thing I know, you're getting kidnapped and shot at. I'm about to assign you a permanent babysitter."

We were in Alden now. Rian had flown to me so she could get a good look at me herself. It didn't matter that I felt like I was losing myself even when I wanted to do so. But at least I had my friends at my side as I tried to piece together what I had left.

I glowered at Rian. "You're hilarious. I will remind you that my own aunt kidnapped me. If you could refrain from making comments from the peanut gallery, that would be awesome."

Sparrow, who'd flown in to check on me, poured an obscenely large glass of wine for herself and then made me a mocktail. "I'm sorry, love, but she has a point. You were like the worst house guest."

"Hey, weren't you the one bleeding at her pool house?"

Sparrow scoffed. "Look, that was not my fault. Some random asshole got the drop on me."

I lifted a brow and laughed. "Aren't you some kind of like badass Wonder Woman type? Serious martial artist? Security expert?"

She shrugged. "Look, these things happen."

Rian laughed. "Seriously though, are you okay?"

I shrugged. "If you mean physically, then other than bearing possible scars on my wrists from the zip ties, I'm fine. I'm just tired. And kind of down."

Sparrow took a long sip and placed her glass on the countertop gently. "It's not unusual to experience a mild depression after a traumatic experience like that."

I didn't want to think about Roman's or Wilder's dour faces when I returned. No one blamed me of course...except they wore permanent resting judgment faces.

Sparrow licked her bottom lip before asking, "You and Kannon?"

I shook my head.

Rian slapped her hand down on the counter. "Now, wait just a minute here. I have seen security footage of that man. He is fine. Please tell me you at least got some."

"Unfortunately, I got more than I bargained for." I hadn't meant to fall for him. Hell, I'd never been in love before. I thought maybe I'd been in love when I probably had only been infatuated, but with Kannon? I'd never felt like this after breaking up with someone. I'd never felt this shattered or torn apart. "He was right. We only knew each other a short time. How are you supposed to know whether or not you care about someone in no time at all? It's an illusion fed by adrenaline and fear."

Sparrow sighed, rubbing her temples. "Can we just go ahead and say the thing? You're in love with him, and he's in love with you."

"He told me he loved me on the plane. But he still thought walking away was the best thing. I have to accept the situation and move on. Although I'm not exactly sure how I'm going to manage that, and I'm certain this feeling of constantly wanting to cry will be a permanent thing."

Rian reached out and took my hand. "Oh, honey, I'm so sorry."

"I have no one to blame but myself. I don't know. Maybe if I'd had some more experience with love and relationships I wouldn't feel so torn up, I guess." And I knew now that Aunt Rebecca had been a helpful hand in making sure I never knew what true love and affection could be.

"It's not your fault."

I was surprised Sparrow was taking my side.

She huffed. "You put yourself out there. You took a chance, and that's really admirable. Lord knows I haven't done that in a million years."

"I don't know. I wish it didn't hurt quite so bad."

"Sweetheart, if you're not in pain over being heartbroken, then you're not doing it right," Rian said. She said it as if she had experience with that pain, but Rian was good at keeping secrets. I was the open book of the two of us. She didn't share every part of her soul with me, even though I'd tried to get her to open up more. Maybe one day she'd let me in.

Eager to change the subject, I prodded both of them, not going too deep into anything that could hurt. "Rian, what's your deal? What happened to the actor? The one from the movie with Diane Lane about infidelity, right?"

She grinned. "A lady doesn't kiss and tell."

Sparrow coughed. "Bullshit. Tell all."

CARRIE ANN RYAN & NANA MALONE

Rian regaled us with stories of what it was like dating on set. "Look, none of that shit that you do on set is meant to be sexy at all."

Sparrow shook her head. "I know there are people around, but isn't it even a little bit sexy?"

Rian laughed. "No. Honestly, you've got Frank holding the boom mic over your face, trying his darn best not to look at your exposed nipple, which, by the way, your co-star has to strategically lick around."

I sat there, jaw agape. Fascinated. "Wait, he actually *licked* your nipple?"

"Well, I mean it has to look that way. You discuss beforehand what you're actually going to do in the scene. It's like dance moves. Step here, touch here, kiss here, lick there."

I leaned forward. "Oh my God, so that was really his hand on your boob? Squeezing?"

Rian shrugged. "Yup."

"Is that when you guys started getting it on?"

Rian laughed. "No! It's too awkward. And not sexy at all. And if you're smart, you never trust any feelings you're having on set. We didn't get together until after. Besides, he had a girlfriend during filming."

"You're telling me there was no showmance?" It was good to talk about things other than Kannon, and Rian was just the storyteller to lift my mood. I could also go a full twenty seconds without thinking of Kannon while she was talking.

She shook her head. "Nope. But during the movie, they broke up. The long filming hours were too much for her. And she's an actress too, so she gets it, but time apart isn't easy. And then during the press junkets, I don't know, we just connected or something. But that's not going to work out. He's that guy who needs someone around. If I was the kind of girl to follow him from set to set and just be available when he is, we could probably make it work. But I'm not that girl. I've got my own shit going on. It was fun for the month or so while we were traveling to promote *Rebel Cause*, but now? It's done."

"Please tell me there were at least orgasms," Sparrow asked, all ears.

Rian laughed, and I said, "Wow, you're really into this."

Sparrow sighed dramatically. "I don't know about you, but I have been high and dry in the desert for far too long. Rian's story is the only thing keeping me going right now. I've got more angst about sex. I need this in my life."

I laughed along with them. But that one little remark just reminded me that my bed would be empty. It told me that everything I felt with Kannon, under his lips, under his hands, that was over now. The one thing I was happy about was that, for the first time in a long

CARRIE ANN RYAN & NANA MALONE

time, I'd been vulnerable with someone. And I knew that was what I needed to do all the time. I couldn't go back to being closed off. Just a little bit distant, waiting for that rejection. Otherwise, I would never be happy.

It was like Sparrow knew the direction of my thoughts because she said, "Look, he's my boss, and my friend, and my mentor, but Kannon is an idiot. One day he's going to realize that he let the best thing in his life go, and he's going to come crawling back. I hope you make him bleed."

Rian raised her glass. "Hear, hear for making him bleed."

I laughed, knowing it was forced, and I raised my glass. "He's not coming back. Or at least, not coming to Alden. If there was a wishing tree to grant me this one wish and he did come back, I promise, I would make him bleed. And who knows? Maybe I wouldn't even be available."

My girls grinned at me. "Amen, sister. That's what I'm talking about," Sparrow hooted.

Rian lifted a brow. "Really?"

Sparrow shrugged and laughed. "What? It seems appropriate."

Rian just rolled her eyes. "Fine, let's go with amen, sister." Then we clinked glasses.

Except I knew the truth. I couldn't even let my heart hope for something like him coming back, otherwise I would always be on this precipice, waiting for him. Waiting for life to happen to me. And I was done waiting.

I was going to live my life in the moment. Make my own plans. I was going to direct my own destiny.

Chapter 20
KANNON

Regrets are for those who forget to live.

A WEEK AFTER LEAVING PARIS, MY ARM HURT, MY head hurt, and pretty much everything else still ached too, especially my heart. I knew I was an idiot, but how far I had dug myself into this hole was a little ridiculous.

I was home in Los Angeles and a million light years away from my heart. But London was safe and tucked away.

And I was alone. Exactly where I needed to be. I deserved that and more.

I'd hurt her. Maybe if I had been strong enough, she wouldn't have been hurt at all. And if that was the case, maybe there would have been a chance for me to stay with her.

I frowned at that line of thought, knowing it couldn't go anywhere.

She wasn't for me.

She couldn't be.

She'd tell me if something changed with her circumstances within the next month, but other than that, there would be no contact. There couldn't be. Not when she had a whole life in front of her that had nothing to do with me. And I would always be the one in the shadows. The one who took the bullet for my charge.

And I couldn't do that and be with London at the same time.

I still couldn't get her face out of my mind.

It's for the best, I told myself. It had to be.

I needed to change my bandage soon and set up the next job with my team. I was lethargic and unmotivated. I had already checked in on Sparrow and annoyed the hell out of her. She should be fine and was on the mend, but I had almost lost her too, and I wouldn't have been able to live with myself if I had.

I would never tell Sparrow that, or she would kick my ass. She was my friend, my teammate, and she had almost died because of my recklessness.

That was why both of them had gotten hurt, and I would never forgive myself.

A loud banging on the door made me freeze and reach for my gun, only I had already put it in the safe. But I had a few weapons near.

I pulled the knife out of my boot and went to the door.

I was already on edge, but when I looked through the peephole, I cursed and thought about keeping the knife. Instead, I slid it back into my boot and opened the door, preparing for what was eventually going to be my downfall.

Three men stood on the other side of the door, all in suits, one looking a little disheveled, one looking cocky as hell, and the other looking like he would break me.

I knew right away who he was...the king.

The King of fucking Alden.

The two flanking him like the Men in Black were London's other brothers, Breck and Wilder.

"Aren't you going to let us in?" the cocky one asked, and I knew that one was Breck.

The other one, Wilder, didn't live up to his name. He just pushed his way through, silent and brooding. It seemed the wild one was Breck, at least from what I could tell from news outlets. The brothers had been named wrong, or maybe they had been named just right.

"Come right on in, why don't you?" I scoffed, pissed off that they were on my doorstep, and ready for whatever fight came.

"I'm sure you would've invited us in eventually," King Roman said, glancing around my loft.

I was rarely at home. And when I was, it was just to sleep, train, and get ready for the next mission.

It had been that way at my old job and continued as I had built my company.

The only reason I had the place was for storage and to be able to say I had a home. But I didn't really. It was hard even to stay there most days. Phoebe had never been in my home. I'd gotten it after I had lost her.

And I even had a bit of her stuff packed away in the closet, which I'd never again look at. Including that damned box from the nursery.

I'd given most of the things to her family. Her parents hadn't even spoken to me since her death.

But I kept a few things—a few things I didn't need to see.

"Should I fix the punch now or what?"

"I take it you know who we are?" the king asked, his voice cultured, that same coolness I had heard over the phone and in countless media appearances.

He was a hardass, but I supposed that came from ruling a country. I respected Roman, but that didn't mean I had to like him, especially when I saw parts of his sister in his face.

I didn't want to think about London. I couldn't.

"I'm Breck, this is Wilder, and you know the king.

And you must be the asshole who broke our sister's heart," Breck said, leaning against my counter.

I shook my head. "Your aunt did that. I was just there to pick up the pieces," I said.

"Oh, our aunt did a lot," Wilder said. "We're just here to make sure you didn't take advantage of her."

I tightened my jaw. "I didn't."

"So you say," Roman said. "But I know my sister. We all do. And she's not broken merely over our aunt being the treacherous snake that she was. She's quiet. Doesn't tell us much. But we know. And we know you fucking touched our sister."

I met the king's gaze and then pulled my eyes away so I could look at the others.

"She's a grown woman. What we had was consensual. It's over."

"You say it's over, and yet, look at you, sitting here alone in the dark, licking your wounds."

"I'm sorry, but do you actually know anything about me? No, you don't. Feel free to go and self-fornicate," I snapped.

Roman's brow lifted even as the corner of his lip twitched. Breck coughed a laugh before recovering himself, and Wilder, well, his expression didn't change.

"Our sister is in pain. You hurt her. So what the fuck did you do to her?" Wilder asked, his voice not even raising a bit.

"I didn't do anything," I said. "I just told her the truth."

"That you didn't love her?" the king asked.

"What did she tell you?" I asked, my heartbreak reflected in my voice.

"She told us enough," Roman whispered. "But you just told us the rest. You're an idiot."

"Excuse me?" I asked, my gaze going from brother to brother.

"You love our sister, don't you, asshole?" Breck asked, looking down at his phone.

"That's none of your business," I bit out.

"I see that wasn't a no," Wilder said, shaking his head. "Should have just said no if you want us off your dick," he whispered.

I barked out a laugh. "I don't want any of you anywhere near my dick."

Wilder grinned for just a moment before looking over at Breck.

"He sounds almost like you," Wilder said.

"Excuse me? I am one of a kind. Nobody can sound like me. Not even the idiot who broke our sister's heart."

"She's not broken up over me. She'll get over me in a minute."

"If you truly believe that, then you're not worth her," Roman said.

I looked up at Roman. "I wasn't worth her to begin with. She's a princess. Who am I?"

"You're the man who saved our sister," Breck said. But I didn't look over at him.

Instead, I kept my gaze on Roman. "I saved your sister, but she still got hurt."

"I would give you anything you asked for. Thank you for keeping our baby sister alive."

What I wanted to tell him was that I wanted her. I needed her. But trying to tell him he wasn't at liberty to give her to me would not have gone well. Besides, I didn't deserve her. "There's nothing I want. As long as she's safe."

"Liar. I can see it on your face," Roman said. He looked over at his brothers and nodded before turning back to me. "Kannon, our plane leaves in an hour. Be on it if you want to at least apologize for being an asshole or if you want to do something good for yourself and for our sister. It's up to you. We're not going to force you."

"But we *could* force you," Wilder said.

"What the hell?" I asked, taking a step back to look at the three of them.

"All we're saying is we like you. You saved our sister. But you hurt her. You better fix it," Breck said.

"How am I supposed to fix this?" I asked, my heart racing.

"You'll figure it out," the king said slowly. "But if you hurt her again, I have two words for you."

"I'm afraid to guess."

"Diplomatic immunity," he whispered. And chills slid up my spine.

"I'm not good for her," I whispered.

"And that is for her to decide. Not you."

And then the three brothers left me standing there wondering what the fuck I was going to do.

THAT'S HOW I SOMEHOW FOUND MYSELF STANDING in front of a fucking palace.

Roman and Wilder had already left to do their thing, and I stood next to Breck, who just raised a brow at me.

"Still going to remain silent? You spent enough time being that way on the plane."

"There wasn't much to say on the plane."

"At least you showed up. I was pretty sure Wilder was going to truss you up and stuff you in the back if you hadn't."

I looked over at London's brother and frowned, trying to size him up, but I really couldn't. He laughed, and he joked, and he acted like he had not a care in the world, but I had a feeling there was something else beneath the surface.

It seemed there always was when it came to this family.

"What do you want me to say?" I asked.

"That's up to you. Wilder and Roman will probably kill you if you do anything to hurt her."

"And you?"

Something dark came over his eyes, and he shook his head. "You won't know what I plan to do in advance."

"You know what I do for a living, don't you? And you're threatening me?" I asked, confused by this man.

"I know exactly what you do, Kannon Adams. I know exactly who you are. I also know that you protected my sister and that she loves you. So don't fuck this up. Now, come into the palace, and we can show you how the royals live."

"I don't think I'm ready for this."

"Nobody ever is. But we're the Waterfords, the royals of Alden."

We made our way through the castle, and I could barely take it all in. It was large, clean, and people seemed to be moving about all the time as if they had places to go and a right to be there. This was where London lived? No wonder she wanted to travel the world and look through her camera lens. This wasn't what she wanted, this life that seemed to be closing in around her.

But I didn't think she had a choice.

And yet somehow, I needed to make her see that I could be a choice for her.

"Okay, here she is. Don't fuck it up." Breck practically pushed me through a set of doors to a courtyard and then closed them behind me.

I looked over my shoulder while Breck saluted before walking away. I turned around, noticing the trees and the flowers and benches everywhere. It seemed to be a private area, with only one person in attendance.

London. She was turned away from me, her hair flowing down her back, and she stood in front of a fountain, her shoulders set, looking regal, like she was set in stone.

I moved closer, one step, and then another.

And London whirled, her eyes wide, her face pale and bruises still evident, and she just looked at me and blinked.

"Kannon?" she asked. She took a step forward, but then she seemed to remember our last meeting and froze.

"London."

"What are you doing here?" she asked with a frown.

"I wanted to talk to you."

She shook her head. "Why? Why do you want to

talk to me? You're the one who pushed me away." She held up her hand. "No, I don't want to rehash that. I don't want to feel like I did before. How did you even get here?"

I was determined to be honest. "Your brothers found me and brought me here. And Breck practically pushed me into this courtyard." I cringed as her face paled even more, but I continued. "I would have found my own way here sooner or later, but I was too chicken shit to take the first step and I needed time to collect my thoughts."

She blinked in disbelief, and I didn't blame her. "I'm going to ask again. *Why* are you here?"

"Because I was an idiot."

"I'm not going to correct you there. You are an idiot. About many things. But why don't you tell me exactly what you mean?"

"You're not going to make this easy, are you?"

"Why should I? I don't even know what this is." London let out a breath, and then she narrowed her eyes at my arm. "How is your arm? Are you okay? I'll get back to being annoyed with you in a minute, but you were literally sliced open a week ago. Should you even be here? How did you even travel?"

I took a step forward and reached out to brush my knuckle against her jaw, but she took a step away. I ignored the hurt I felt. After all, I'd earned it.

"I'm fine. It's not the first time."

She swallowed hard, tears swelling in her eyes before she blinked them away and rage filled them instead. Good, she was still the fiery London I had fallen for.

I just hoped to hell she could forgive me.

"I'm so sorry."

"You said that, but you haven't told me why you're sorry."

"I'll never get the picture of you hurt and bleeding out of my mind. And it's my fault that you were even hurt to begin with."

"How could you blame yourself for that? My aunt orchestrated all of this so that she could have the throne for her son. And yet you're blaming yourself? You did everything to protect me. I'm the one who ran out because I couldn't stand to look at you."

"And if I hadn't pushed you away, if I hadn't acted like a dick because I was scared about what I was feeling for you and my own inadequacies, maybe you wouldn't have run straight into danger. Maybe neither you nor Sparrow would have been hurt."

"Is she really okay? She and I have been texting a bit, but I don't know if she's lying to me or not."

"You're checking up on her?" I asked.

"Of course, I am. She was hurt because of me."

"No she wasn't. None of this was your fault."

"Then none of this was your fault either," she shouted back.

I hadn't even realized I had raised my voice until she did the same.

"I'm going to be honest and tell you that I'm scared," I said, not even realizing the words were coming out of my mouth until I'd spoken them. I just needed to get my head out of my ass and say what I was feeling.

"Scared of what?" she asked wearily.

"I was scared you were going to end up like Phoebe."

She pressed her lips together. "You loved her very much," she whispered, and I heard the pain there.

I stepped forward again, this time hesitantly putting my hand on her cheek. She didn't move away, and I took that as a good sign. "I did. I loved her very much. But that doesn't mean she's the only person I can ever love."

"What are you saying, Kannon?"

"I'm saying that sometimes I get in my own way. I do it all the time. Phoebe's not the only one in my heart now. And that means I'm going to be scared to death of losing you like I lost her."

"Kannon," she breathed. Then she pushed my hand away. "I bared myself to you, and you threw it back in my face."

I let out a breath, the hurt in her words a visceral

pain. "I know, and that's unforgivable. I was trying to do what I thought was best for you."

"You were trying to make my decisions for me. Something that everyone has done for me since the time I was conceived. Most likely, before that. How do I know you won't throw that back in my face again?"

"You don't. You'll have to trust me. And I'll have to spend however long it takes working to make sure I earn that trust."

"I shouldn't even be listening to this. I should let you walk away again or do it myself." I waited for her to continue, waited to hear something that would give me hope. "But...I can't. If I do that, I'll only be hurting myself. And I'm done hurting my future and heart just to live up to everyone else's expectations."

I nearly fell to my knees, truly ready to grovel. "I'm sorry. I'm scared. I was an idiot. I'll do whatever you want. But take me back. I know this is too fast, and there's so much left in our way, but let's figure it out together. I'll go down on my knees if I have to. I'll grovel. I'll do anything you want. But just forgive me for walking away. Forgive me, please."

She blinked up at me and then reached up and traced her finger along my jawline.

I leaned into her touch, soaking it in. I didn't want this to be the last time she touched me.

"You're right. It's far too fast," she whispered. "But I

know what I'm feeling. I don't know how this is going to work. I don't even know what my future looks like beyond this moment, but I know I don't want to have that future without you. I want to figure it out. I love you, Kannon. I wasn't lying or caught up in the moment when I said it."

I sucked in a breath. "And I love you too," I whispered. Her eyes filled with tears, and I leaned in and brushed my lips along hers. She sank into me, and I nearly groaned. I'd missed this connection between us.

I didn't know what was ahead of us, but I knew this needed to be part of it.

"I don't know what I need to do for this to work, but I'm all in. There's just going to be a lot of threads to untangle and weave for us to make it work."

Her eyes clouded for a moment, and she backed away but took my hand in hers. "You're right. I have no idea how this is going to work. And I don't want any promises beyond this moment. But I love you, and I want to figure it out, even though we have a lot of obstacles to overcome. My kingdom still has that arcane law we have to deal with, and my timing couldn't be worse." She cringed and put her hand on her stomach.

My eyes widened. "Do you know this soon?" I asked, fear and what felt like elation tangling up together.

She shook her head, her hand falling. "No, it's far

too early to tell, and as I said, I'm on birth control. But that doesn't negate the fact that there's still a rule in place that states if I don't get pregnant, or if my brothers don't impregnate someone else within the next few months, we could lose our throne. And then, even if we get around that, I'm still the princess. I still have responsibilities. And you have your job to deal with, and I have my photography career, and... I just don't know."

I pressed my lips to hers, kissed her hard, and then pulled away, resting my forehead against hers. "We'll figure it out together. I have some of the best people in the business when it comes to figuring out tricky scenarios. And your family is pretty damn smart, too." There was a pointed cough, and I turned, pushing London behind me.

She pushed at me and laughed. "You don't need to protect me here. It's just my brother."

The King of Alden walked from behind a tree and raised a brow.

"While I do enjoy the fact that you're so protective you'd put yourself in front of my sister, I don't know if I need you guys to make out like that in public."

"We're hardly in public. These are my private gardens."

"So private that you didn't even notice me here?"

"That won't be a mistake I make again," I bit out through gritted teeth.

The King of Alden nodded and chuckled. "Good. As for the issues regarding the royal line?" the King asked, shaking his head. "I've got a plan. Just don't fuck this up between the two of you."

"Roman," London began, but he shook his head.

"Don't. I've got it handled, just like I said I would. Live your life, London. Live it the way you've always wanted but have never been able to. I'm your big brother. I'll always protect you." He paused and looked at me. "You just do the same thing, or I'll end you."

"Understood." I said, at the same time London shouted, "Roman!"

I laughed and pulled London close. "Let him protect you. And let me do the same."

"My God, it's like you guys don't understand I can walk on two feet."

"Oh, we do, but we still get to be the big growly men," the king said before he walked away with a purposeful stride.

I had no idea what he was about to do, but I had a feeling it might rock the country of Alden for years to come.

I turned to London and let out a breath.

"So now what?" I asked.

"I don't know. But I guess we'd better figure it out."

As I leaned into her and took her mouth with mine,

I knew we were far from figuring out our futures, far from finding our paths.

But we had taken a step, and we had found our way to each other.

And that, I supposed, was the point of a future. Even if it scared the hell out of me.

Chapter 21
LONDON

Always expect the unexpected.

1 Month Later

I let out a long breath.

"Okay. Here goes nothing."

"I feel like I'm going to throw up," Kannon said from behind me, and I glared over my shoulder.

"You just held my hair back after I threw up. Am I going to have to do the same for you?"

"You're welcome to try, princess."

I smiled at that, even though I was still slightly

nauseated. The idea of him calling me princess wasn't so bad anymore.

It just gave me hope, made me feel loved and warm. I must be losing my mind.

"I can't believe we're bonding over vomit," I said. "Not very romantic."

Kannon shrugged. "You agreed to be mine. That means you don't get the romance."

I rolled my eyes. "Sure, whatever you say. You're totally not romantic."

"I'm not. I will not rely on social norms where I have to suddenly be a romantic duke or any of that shit."

"You are not a duke, Kannon. Far from it."

"Well I don't know now; Duke Kannon sounds pretty good. Or maybe another title. Knight? Oh nice, Knight Kannon."

"You turned down my brother when he offered to knight you, so don't get sad that you're not one now. Though it does have a ring to it."

Kannon just shook his head. "Are we really going to not look down at this moment and just keep talking about trivial things that mean nothing? Because I can continue to do that. I can also bring Sparrow in, and she can talk your ear off while we forget what we're supposed to be thinking about."

"Maybe you should do that. Maybe we should forget

any of this is happening and just go out to the family dinner and not know."

Kannon turned me around so that I was facing him, and he cupped my cheek, brushing his lips along mine.

"Darling, princess of mine, I love you. Whatever happens, I'm here. We started this journey a little off, and we both know it. But we're here. We're finding our way. I love you. And if what we think is about to happen happens, then we'll deal with it together."

"I just don't know if I'm ready."

"I don't know if I'm ready either. But I think whoever says that they're ready is just full of themselves."

"Oh that's so sweet." I moaned, getting a little lightheaded.

Kannon sat me down on the lid of the toilet and brushed my hair back from my face.

"You need me to hold your hair back again?" he asked, worry in his tone. He was always worried when I got lightheaded these days. I had a feeling he was going to get a whole lot worse if what happened next truly changed everything.

"Look at it, Kannon. You tell me." I kept my eyes closed, afraid I was going to throw up.

Again.

Keeping my eyes tightly shut, I handed over the stick and was grateful when Kannon took it from me.

"Okay, here we go in three, two, one."

My eyes were shut, so I didn't know if he reacted. He was just so damn silent. He was far too good at that.

"Kannon? Talk to me."

"Open your eyes, babe."

I shook my head. "Nope. Not going to do it."

"Really? This is the line you're going to draw in the sand right now?" he asked, deadpan.

"Just tell me."

"Okay, how about I tell you this. It turns out that little law of your country isn't going to matter, because you are about to provide an heir."

My eyes shot open, and I nearly fell off the toilet seat. Kannon dropped the pregnancy stick, and it clattered, echoing in the large bathroom as he dropped to his knees in front of me, leaning in closer.

He kissed me, and I leaned into him, needing him.

"I love you so much," he whispered.

"Always," I gasped.

Then he tugged me into the shower, and I fell for him all over again.

Afterward, both of us somewhat sated, I watched the man I loved stand behind me in the mirror as he fixed his tie and I put in my earrings.

"We're going to be parents."

"The phrase *holy shit* comes to mind," he said.

"I guess so."

"Are you okay?" he asked, his eyes on mine in the mirror.

"I don't know. We always knew it was a possibility, especially when I started getting sick recently."

"True, but it did happen out of nowhere. And it is early."

"I know. But I love you, and we're going to figure this out. Even if we did things a little bit out of order."

"Out of order works. We don't want to be conventional, do we, princess?" he asked, then he leaned down and kissed my bare shoulder.

We weren't engaged; we weren't married. But it would happen. Probably sooner rather than later because an illegitimate heir to the throne, even if they would be further down the line than any of Roman's future children, wouldn't be great.

So if Kannon didn't get on one knee soon, I would have to be the one who did so. But that was fine. Like he said, we liked being unconventional, even if we were sometimes set in those truly conventional ways.

"Do we tell your family?" he asked.

"Normally I would say it's far too early, but with Roman and Breck and Wilder working so hard on finding a loophole, maybe we should. I don't think we can wait." I paused, looking at Kannon again.

"What is it?" he asked, his voice solemn.

"I know this isn't what you signed up for."

"Princess, it's exactly what I signed up for."

I snorted, shaking my head, far more emotional than I had been before.

I'd have liked to blame it on the hormones, but I had a feeling it had more to do with the shock of my aunt trying to kill me, and finding Kannon, and everything happening all at once.

It was hard to wrap my head around everything, and I was still working on it.

And now there was one more thing rocking my whole world.

I put my hand over my belly and sighed. This little baby would change everything, and I was already in love with them.

Far more than I thought possible.

"We'll tell your brothers tonight," Kannon said. "And that will be the last of their input."

That made me throw my head back and laugh, and I leaned into Kannon's touch.

"Oh, you're so cute if you think that's actually what's going to happen. If you think my brothers give you the stink eye now for daring to touch their precious little princess baby sister? Oh, it's going to get so bad when they learn I'm pregnant."

"They're going to wrap you up in cotton wool. You do know that, right?."

I cringed. "You're right. I guess we need to tell them

and then run away together." I grinned, and Kannon gave me a wide smile.

"Where do you want to run away to, princess?" he asked, his voice a low deep purr.

It sent shivers down my back, and though we had already sated ourselves in the shower, I wanted another round.

Maybe I could blame it on the hormones, but no, it was all Kannon.

"Anywhere you want to go. As long as I'm with you and I have my camera, it makes no difference to me. We'll figure it out."

"I'm still not letting you take pictures of me naked," Kannon said, and I burst out laughing.

"That was in your head. I'm not the one who offered."

"So now you don't want to take pictures of me naked?" Kannon asked as he helped me off my stool.

"You're a menace."

"I'm your menace," Kannon said.

"Okay, let's go tell my brothers."

"And let the true menace begin."

I smiled, knowing I was in perfectly good hands. Not just Kannon's, but mine.

We made our way through the palace toward the family dining room where my brothers would be.

We were having some of Kannon's team over, as well as a few of my brothers' friends.

But first, it would just be my three brothers, because we were starting early.

It was time we figured out how to make it in this new dynamic of ours without our Aunt Rebecca, knowing that her deep betrayal would sting for years to come.

I would never get over what she had done, knowing I had put my trust in the wrong person, but I would learn to find who I needed to be again. And now, I wouldn't have to do it alone. I would have Kannon, my brothers, Rian, and all my friends. I didn't need Rebecca.

And I could move past that point in my life. Eventually.

My brothers were all in the dining room, each holding a glass of wine or liquor of some sort in their hands.

They were glaring at one another before Breck burst out laughing, Roman shook his head, and Wilder rolled his eyes.

I loved them so much.

They were overbearing, overprotective, and would be until the end of my days, but they were family. And now I had a family of my own.

"There she is," Breck said. "Took you long enough."

He glared over at Kannon. "You know, she used to be on time for everything. Now she's late all the time."

I bristled. "You guys were horribly early. It's like you decided to meet up before the scheduled time. Did you?"

Roman shook his head before the others could speak. "It was by chance. However, I did get to tell them something that concerns you."

"What?" I asked, a sense of foreboding sliding over me.

"I heard back from the Council of Lords."

I opened my mouth to say something, but Roman continued quickly.

"It's over. The royal line will remain the same. Children will come when they come. If they do. But we will not be forced into anything."

I met Roman's gaze, elation and something else twisting inside me. Something had happened, something I didn't know. Something that had passed between my brothers.

"What did you give up, Roman?" I asked, my voice quiet.

He just gave me a tight smile and shook his head. "Nothing that wasn't easily given," he said softly.

"Can you take it back?" I blurted, and Kannon squeezed my hand.

"Why would we want to?" Roman asked softly. Almost too softly.

"We're pregnant. We're having a baby."

Wilder took a step back, while Breck just blinked and burst out laughing.

But I saw the look on Roman's face.

The look of shock and something else. His jaw tensed ever so slightly, but then he smiled, and his eyes filled with some emotion I couldn't read.

Something had happened, and I didn't know what to do.

But instead of saying anything, he set his drink down, took three strides closer to me, and cupped my face.

"My baby sister's having a baby of her own. Congratulations." Then he kissed my forehead and looked up at Kannon. "I'll kill you if you hurt her."

"We know where to hide the bodies," Wilder said.

"And I'm good at driving a getaway car," Breck added.

"Really? This is what you're going to talk about over our announcement?" I asked, exasperated.

"They're your brothers; it's what I expected," Kannon said. Then my brothers hugged me and congratulated Kannon while giving him a dirty look.

Yes, an engagement would have to come soon, but

not tonight. Tonight I was with my family and Kannon, and the baby growing in my womb.

I had never known if I was ready to be a mother, and now I would only have a few more months to figure it out.

But in the end, I had Kannon, and I was so excited to see what would happen.

I'd found my happiness, and not just with Kannon, not just in the future of our child.

But in who I could be and who I could rely on.

I was the Princess of Alden, the love of Kannon's life. I was London Waterford. And I was happy.

Epilogue
SPARROW

Always a commoner. Never a Princess.
Just how I like it.

FOR A WHILE, I HONESTLY HADN'T THOUGHT THE two lovebirds in front of me would be able to get their shit together.

As I watched Kannon and London waltz across the ballroom, I couldn't help but get the warm fuzzies. Not that I was particularly one for warm fuzzy feelings, but if anyone deserved that kind of love, it was Kannon. And London. True to her word, she had made him grovel. Which I was all about. She was good for him and kept him on his toes.

The best thing about their union was that it meant that Kannon Security was going international. Kannon wanted to open offices in Alden, and eventually, Paris. Which meant more staff. It also meant I was required to train said staff, meaning more travel for me.

I didn't hate that one bit. Some thought that perhaps Kannon would become lead security for the royal family, and that might occur later, but for now, it was all about compromise and finding what worked for the two of them. London was moving to Los Angeles where we were based. LA could serve just as well as a launching point for photography assignments as Alden could, and I was thrilled to have her close. We'd get to hang out more, and I'd have estrogen in my life again. And since Rian was often in LA for work, I'd get some quality girl time. Not quite as much hanging out with the boys at the weekly poker game. I hadn't realized until we'd been hanging out recently that I'd desperately missed girl time.

I glanced around the ballroom, looking for Rian to say goodnight. The ceremony had been the most beautiful thing I'd ever seen, held in the gardens surrounded by flowers and overlooking the ocean. And the reception was the kind of fun you read about in magazines. Champagne flowed, and they had one of the hottest DJs from the Ibiza circuits do their reception. Not that Kannon had any idea who he was, but he'd been a present from

Rian, who refused to have bad, boring music at the reception.

However, my feet were killing me. And though the doctor had cleared me for duty, I still had to take it easy. My side was healing well, but every now and then, if I overdid it or stood too long, I got fatigued.

When I found Rian, she was surrounded by a group of people, each and every one of them enthralled by the actress. And honestly, it was difficult *not* to be. With her deep brown skin and her brilliant white smile, her coiling curls that flowed and bounced down her back, full lips, wide almond-shaped eyes, and the kind of cheekbones most people paid their plastic surgeons for, she was stunning. But she was also warm and open and gregarious.

I also noticed how Roman, London's oldest brother and the King of Alden, stared at her. He was doing it surreptitiously too. He would steal a quick glance, frown at her, and then turn back to his conversation. But every time she laughed, he'd look in her direction and scowl.

What the hell was going on there? I knew Rian and London had been friends for a while, so maybe the two had a history I wasn't aware of. I'd met Roman and one of her other brothers, Wilder. Wilder was stern and glowered even more than Roman did, but I liked them both. The other one, Breck, I hadn't seen yet. I'd come in just in time for the rehearsal, and he'd had an assignment away from the party. So I'd probably see him at the family brunch in the morning. All of London's brothers were that sort of aristocratic drop-dead gorgeous type. You could tell they were brothers with their sharp jawlines and patrician noses. And also their eyes, the set of them, with those thick lashes. They were brothers, all right.

When it looked like Rian would be busy for a while, I shot a quick text to her and London, knowing full well that London wouldn't check her messages for a while.

Sparrow: *You guys look amazing. My side hurts. I'm going to crash. I'll see you in the morning for the brunch.*

I gave Olly a wave as he twirled some brunette across the dance floor. He winked in return with a smile. He was having a blast. Good for him. Kannon had been relying on both of us a lot with things changing so much. Olly needed time off just as much as I did.

As I left the ballroom, I gave some smiles and nods and waves to people I'd met during my stay. I hoped my tight smile said I'd had a great time and not, *"Dear God, if you talk to me, I'm so tired I might bite your head off."*

All I wanted to do was crash and get off my damn feet. Right outside the ballroom doors, I slid my shoes off. I knew it was probably a major faux pas, but hell, my feet were killing me. The moment I slipped them off, I felt so much better—the cool marble floor icing down the inflammation.

I pulled the little map out of my dress pocket. Nothing better than a dress with pockets and a map to show me the way. The map in the party favors London had given her bridal party was a brilliant touch because it was the only way I'd be able to find my way back to my room. The palace was massive. Even after being there for three days, I was still unable to find the correct hallway toward my quarters, and I was trained for shit like that. I kept worrying that eventually I'd stumble down to the dungeons and no one would ever find me again.

Although London kept trying to tell me dungeons didn't exist in the palace, I wasn't sure if I should believe her or not. I mumbled to myself as I turned left down the hall and then took a right past the gardens.

One more right turn, and I was in my hallway. I recognized the painting right across from my room which I'd drawn as the X that marked the spot on my map.

London's family had graduated to the tech of the new century, and so had their digs. As I approached my door, my phone told the door who I was, and the lock disengaged.

Turning the handle, I pushed on the heavy wood but paused when I heard moaning.

What the hell? I pushed the door farther, letting in more light, and the moaning increased. Then somebody called out, "Love, whether you're joining us or not, letting in the light is kind of rude."

"What the fuck?"

I hit the lights, only to find a man in my damn bed. A man with the nicest ass I'd ever seen. In my bed. With a blonde and a redhead.

"Are you fucking kidding me? This is where I'm sleeping tonight."

His grin was rakish. "Go ahead, strip down. Join us."

Whiskey. Tango. Foxtrot. "Oh my God. You're a pig." I briskly turned, struggling with the heavy door, which gave him time to catch me. He had the sheet held at his waist as the women in bed grumbled.

"Wait." The heat from his body was hot enough to scald. And his voice, low and slightly slurring, sent a shiver down my entire body.

His hand grabbed my forearm, and I shook him off as I managed to get the door open. "No, thank you. Don't touch me. I can see where your hands have been." He was lucky I wasn't in the mood to hurt my side or cause a scene, or I'd have thrown him over my shoulder and taught him what happened when someone touched me without permission.

He glanced back at the bed and laughed. "You're the one who tried to join our private celebration."

I could smell the alcohol on his breath. And from the dim light in the foyer, I could see that his pupils were dilated. Jesus Christ, how trashed was he?

And I knew *exactly* who this was. Hard to miss it when he looked so much like his fucking brothers.

Breck Waterford. The partier of the family without a care in the world.

Wilder was the one with the connections and the focus.

Roman was the one with steel and responsibility.

Breck? He looked to be just like his cousin Barkley. *Useless.*

"No, you idiot. This is *my* room. You don't even recognize me, do you?"

He leaned closer. "Oh, I recognize you all right. You're my sister's uptight little friend. The stiff one who's always a little too watchful, who sees too much."

"Well, I've certainly seen enough tonight. Let go of my arm, or I will put you down."

He leered down at me. "Now that, I would like to see."

With a well-practiced judo move, I placed a hand over the one still holding me, swung the arm he was holding around, and then pressed down on his wrist. He winced and immediately released me. "Jesus, fuck."

"I told you not to touch me."

CARRIE ANN RYAN & NANA MALONE

He held up his hands. "Fine. All you had to do was ask."

"You're a dick."

He grinned. "Oh, you haven't even seen the worst of it."

"Touch me again, and you'll be missing your appendage."

"I promise, I'm not going to touch you again until you ask me."

I leaned forward so he could hear me as I ground out each word. "I will never ask you to touch me."

"Never say never, love."

****

Next Up in the Tattered Royals series?
ENEMY HEIR
For more information please go to Carrie Ann Ryan and Nana Malone's websites.

Want to read a special BONUS EPILOGUE featuring Kannon & London? CLICK HERE!

A Note from Carrie Ann & Nana

Thank you so much for reading **ROYAL LINE!!**

Next up from in the Tattered Royals series is ENEMY HEIR! Sparrow and Beck might not be ready for each other, but we're ready for them!

The Tattered Royals Series:

Book 1: Royal Line

Book 2: Enemy Heir

More to come!

WANT TO READ A SPECIAL BONUS EPILOGUE FEATURING KANNON & LONDON? CLICK HERE!

Acknowledgments

Writing a book is never easy. Writing a book with your friend is honestly a lot more fun! At least that's what I'm telling myself. Please, Nana, don't disabuse me of this notion!

Nana and I would love to thank so many people for helping us get Royal Line completed!

Thank you to our editors, Angie and Chelle, for somehow making Royal Line into a full book and not just fun times with Kannon and London where they fight and have steamy interludes.

Thank you to our amazing cover artist, Jaycee for not only hitting this cover out of the park, but for doing it on the first try. Thank you to Wander and Kaz for this fantastic image!

Thank you to our friends who are numerous in

name and even more so in knowledge and genius! We couldn't do this without you as our touchstones.

I (Carrie Ann - the louder one) would love to thank my family for being so supportive during this book. Thank you for your help and for not laughing when I said I wanted to write about princesses who kicked butt.

I (Nana - the one with all the hair) would like to thank Carrie for making this whole process so much fun. This series is going to be such a wild ride.

And thank you dear readers for being so fantastic! Here is to more royals!

~Carrie Ann & Nana

About the Author

Carrie Ann Ryan and Nana Malone have been writing romances for over a decade. Between them, they have nearly two hundred romances under their belt to date!

That means they love romance, happy ever afters, and growly heroes, and the idea that love is love is love.

They were fangirls first, then friends, and now writing partners. Their Tattered Royals series is just the start...and they can't wait to see what comes next.

Find out more at each of their websites:

www.CarrieAnnRyan.com

https://nanamaloneromance.net/

Also from Carrie Ann & Nana Malone

With nearly two hundred heart pounding and thrilling romances between them, they figured they'd show you the best place to start with both of their works!

Loved Royal Line? This is where to go next:

From Carrie Ann & Nana:
The Tattered Royals Series:

Book 1: Royal Line
Book 2: Enemy Heir
More to come!

Start here if you'd like to read Carrie Ann Ryan:
The Montgomery Ink: Boulder Series:

Book 1: Wrapped in Ink

Book 2: Sated in Ink

Book 3: Embraced in Ink

Book 4: Seduced in Ink

Book 4.5: Captured in Ink

Start here if you'd like to read Nana Malone:
The See No Evil Trilogy:

Book 1: Big Ben

Book 2: The Benefactor

Book 3: For Her Benefit